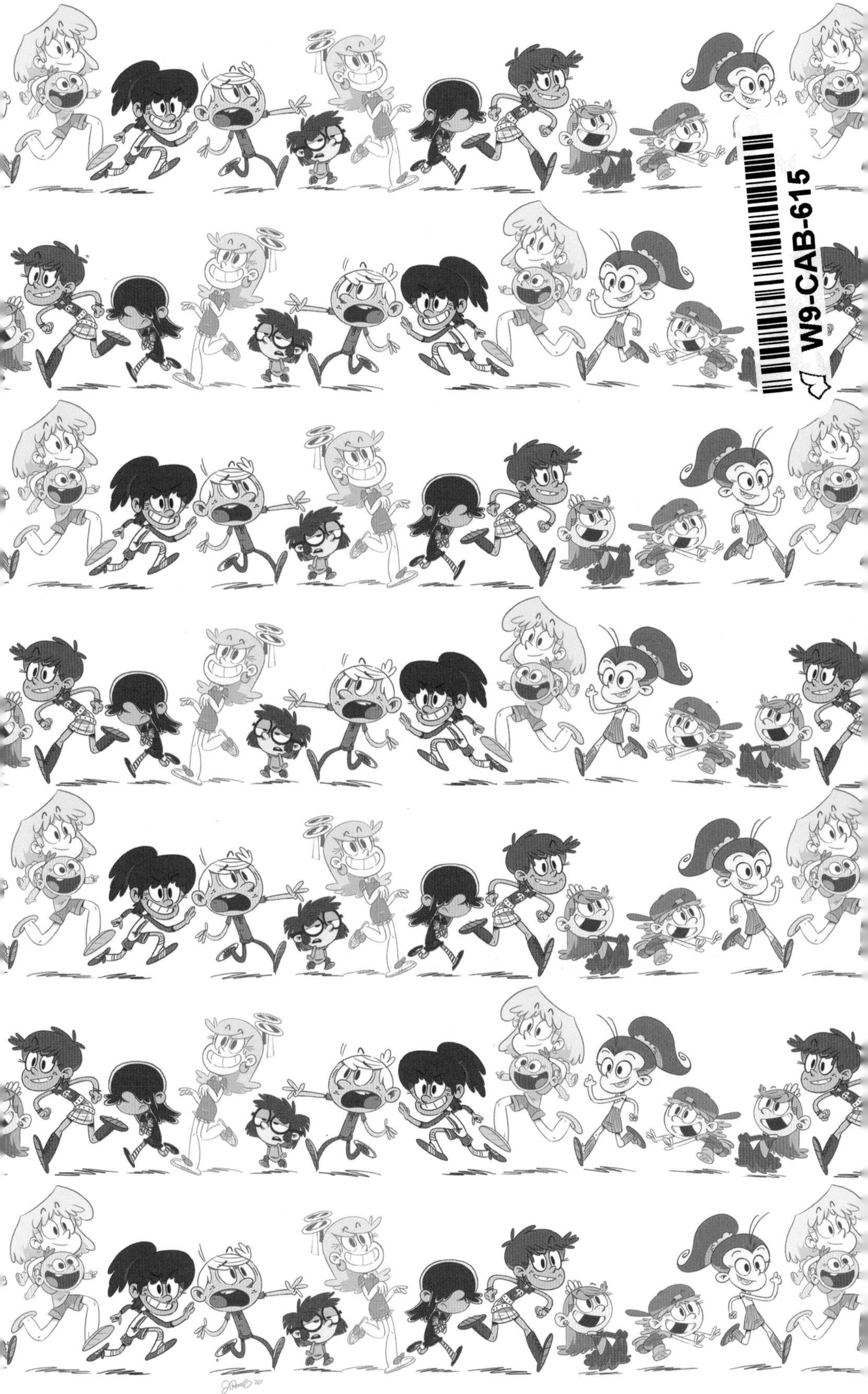

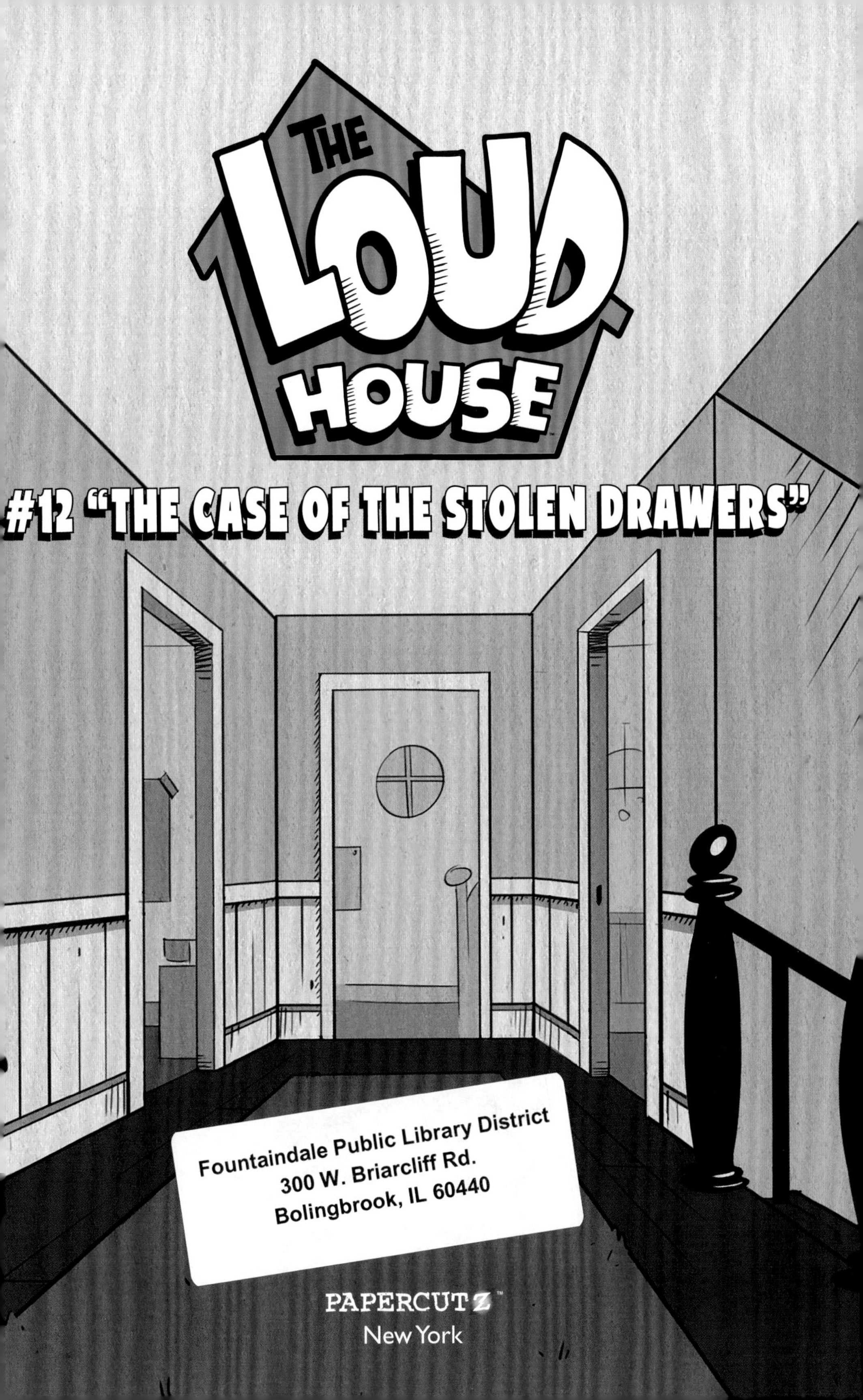

The Loud House

#12 "The Case of the Stolen Drawers"

PAPERCUTZ
New York

nickelodeon GRAPHIC NOVELS AVAILABLE FROM PAPERCUTZ

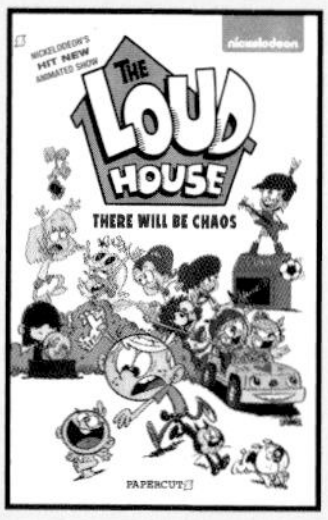
The Loud House
There Will Be Chaos
THE LOUD HOUSE
#1
"There Will Be Chaos"

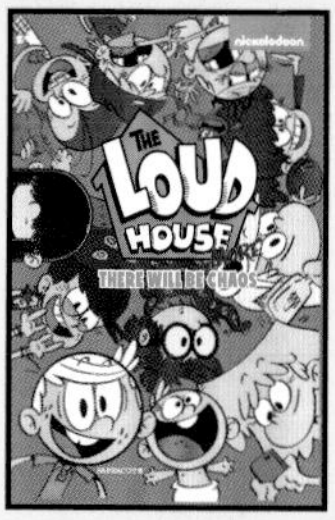
The Loud House
There Will Be Chaos
THE LOUD HOUSE
#2
"There Will Be More Chaos"

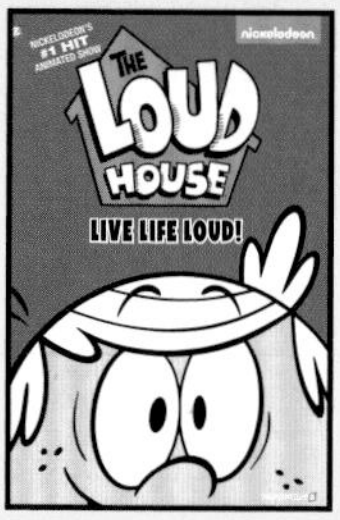
The Loud House
Live Life Loud!
THE LOUD HOUSE
#3
"Live Life Loud!"

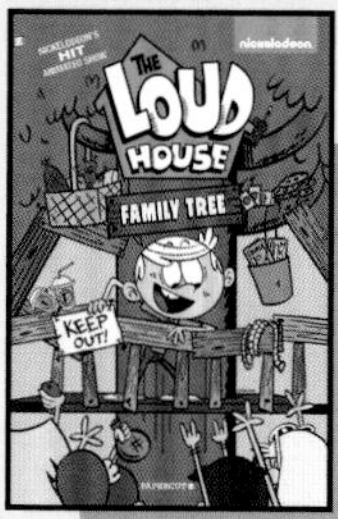
The Loud House
Family Tree
Keep Out!
THE LOUD HOUSE
#4
"Family Tree"

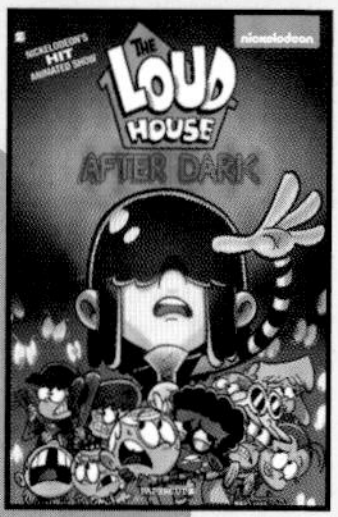
The Loud House
After Dark
THE LOUD HOUSE
#5
"After Dark"

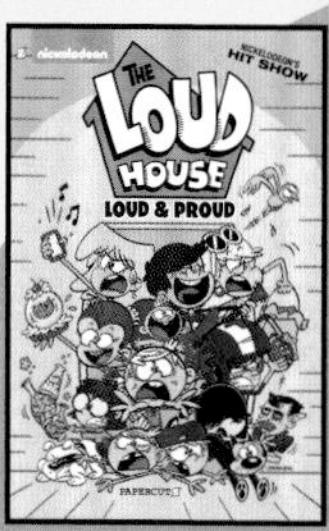
The Loud House
Loud & Proud
THE LOUD HOUSE
#6
"Loud and Proud"

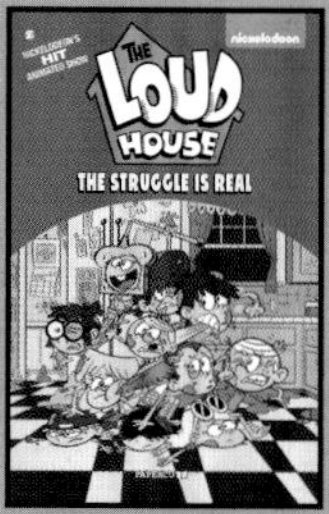
The Loud House
The Struggle is Real
THE LOUD HOUSE
#7
"The Struggle is Real"

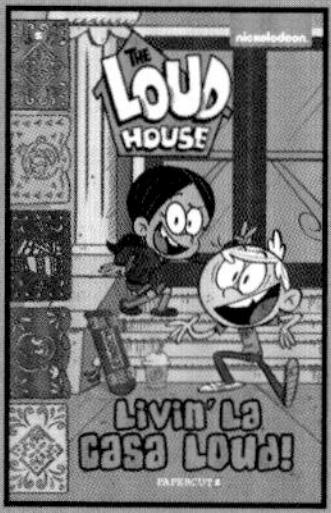
The Loud House
Livin' La Casa Loud!
THE LOUD HOUSE
#8
"Livin' La Casa Loud"

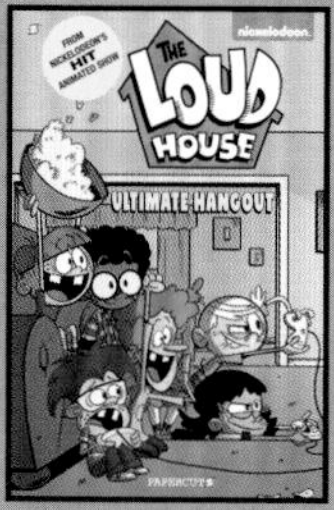
The Loud House
Ultimate Hangout
THE LOUD HOUSE
#9
"Ultimate Hangout"

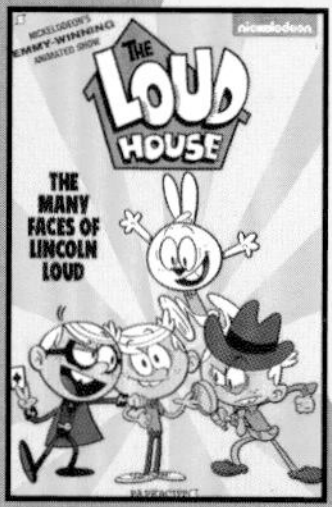
The Loud House
The Many Faces of Lincoln Loud
THE LOUD HOUSE
#10
"The Many Faces of Lincoln Loud"

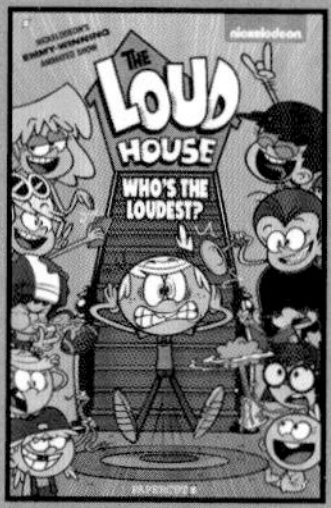
The Loud House
Who's the Loudest?
THE LOUD HOUSE
#11
"Who's the Loudest?"

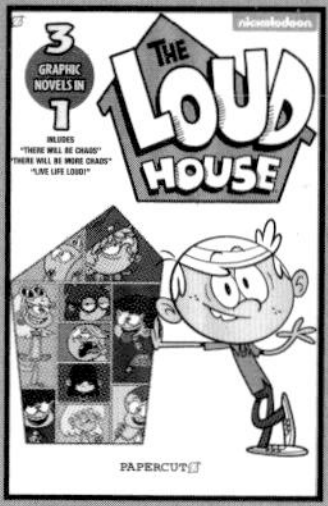
3 Graphic Novels in 1
The Loud House
THE LOUD HOUSE
3 IN 1
#1

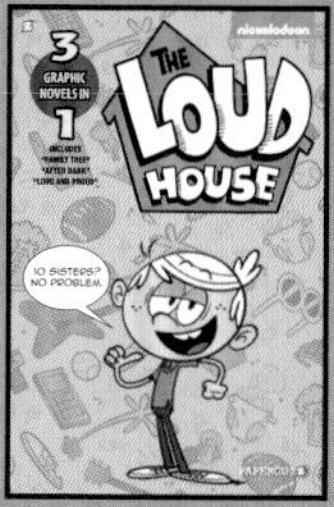
3 Graphic Novels in 1
The Loud House
10 sisters? No problem.
THE LOUD HOUSE
3 IN 1
#2

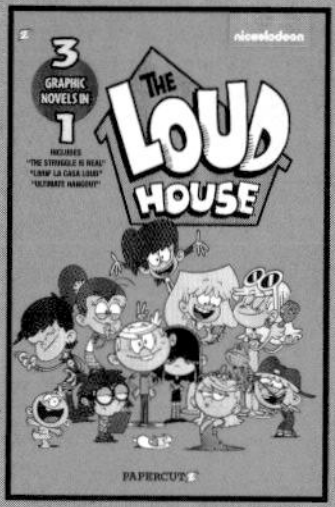
3 Graphic Novels in 1
The Loud House
THE LOUD HOUSE
3 IN 1
#3

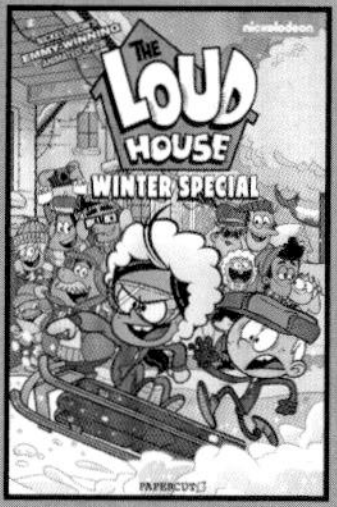
The Loud House
Winter Special
THE LOUD HOUSE
WINTER SPECIAL

COMING SOON

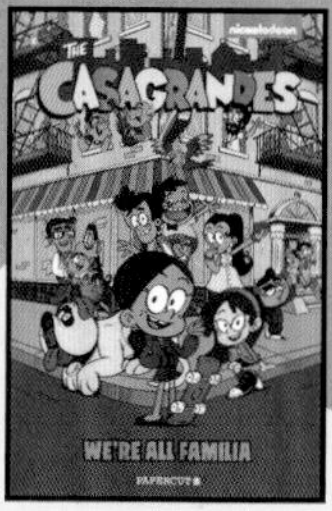
The Casagrandes
We're All Familia
THE CASAGRANDES
#1
"We're All Familia"

COMING SOON

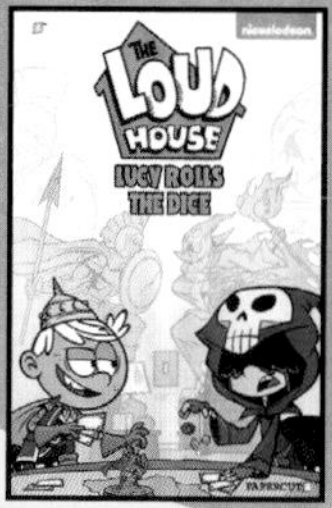
The Loud House
Lucy Rolls the Dice
THE LOUD HOUSE
#13
"Lucy Rolls the Dice"

COMING SOON

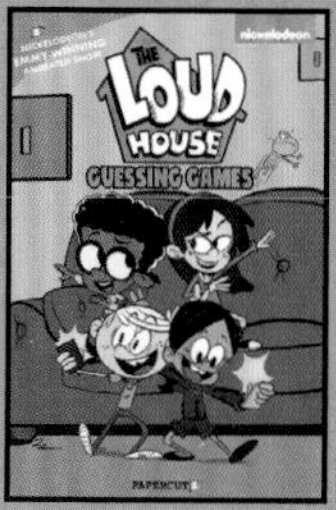
The Loud House
Guessing Games
THE LOUD HOUSE
#14
"Guessing Games"

COMING SOON

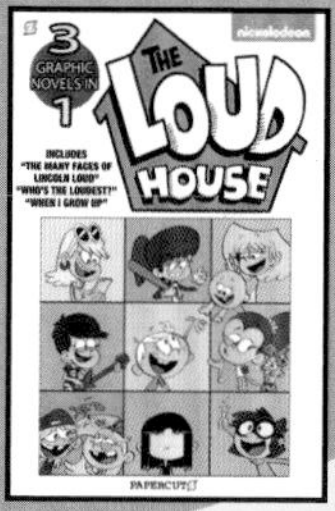
3 Graphic Novels in 1
The Loud House
THE LOUD HOUSE
3 IN 1
#4

COMING SOON

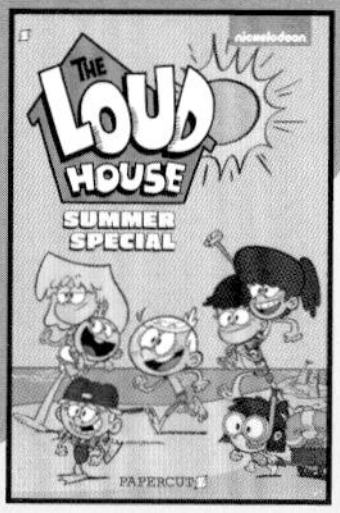
The Loud House
Summer Special
THE LOUD HOUSE
SUMMER SPECIAL

The Loud House and The Casagrandes graphic novels and specials are available for $7.99 each in paperback, $12.99 each in hardcover. THE LOUD HOUSE 3 IN 1 graphic novels are available for $14.99 each in paperback only.
Available from booksellers everywhere. You can also order online from Papercutz.com, or call 1-800-886-1223, Monday through Friday, 9-5 EST. MC, Visa, and AmEx accepted. To order by mail, please add $5.00 for postage and handling for the first book ordered, $1.00 for each additional book and make check payable to NBM Publishing.
Send to: Papercutz, 160 Broadway, Suite 700, East Wing, New York, NY 10038.

THE LOUD HOUSE

#12 "THE CASE OF THE STOLEN DRAWERS"

nickelodeon THE LOUD HOUSE

#12 "THE CASE OF THE STOLEN DRAWERS"

ACE SAVVY
JUSTICE IN SPADES

"THE CASE OF THE STOLEN DRAWERS"
Kiernan Sjursen-Lien — Writer
Tyler Koberstein — Artist, Colorist
Wilson Ramos Jr. — Letterer

"GOING COCO-NUTS!"
Jair Holguin — Writer
Erin Hunting — Artist, Colorist
Wilson Ramos Jr. — Letterer

"OLLIE OLLIE OXEN FREE"
Jair Holguin — Writer
Zazo Aguiar — Artist, Colorist
Vic Miyuki — Colorist
Wilson Ramos Jr. — Letterer

"TONGUE TIED"
Julia Guillen — Writer
Ron Bradley — Artist, Colorist
Wilson Ramos Jr. — Letterer

"ZACH AND THE MEAN CHALK"
Derek Fridolfs — Writer
Erin Hyde — Artist, Colorist
Wilson Ramos Jr. — Letterer

"COMIC RELIEF"
Caitlin Fein — Writer
Zazo Aguiar — Artist,
Vic Miyuki — Colorist
Wilson Ramos Jr. — Letterer

"LEVEL UP"
Kiernan Sjursen-Lien — Writer
Lee-Roy Lahey — Artist
Peter Bertucci — Colorist
Wilson Ramos Jr. — Letterer

"MEAT YOUR MAKER"
Derek Fridolfs — Writer
George Holguin — Artist
Vic Miyuki — Colorist
Wilson Ramos Jr. — Letterer

"MODEL PETS"
Kacey Wooley-Huang — Writer
Kelsey Wooley — Artist, Colorist
Wilson Ramos Jr. — Letterer

"DIAGNOSIS: LOUD"
Paul Allor — Writer
Melissa Kleynowski — Artist
Princess Bizares — Colorist
Wilson Ramos Jr. — Letterer

"CAKENSTEIN'S MONSTER"
Paul Allor — Writer
Erin Hunting — Artist, Colorist
Wilson Ramos Jr. — Letterer

"LUCY'S SUMMER FASHION TIPS" from THE LOUD HOUSE SUMMER SPECIAL
Caitlin Fein — Writer
Max Alley — Artist
Peter Bertucci — Colorist
Wilson Ramos Jr. — Letterer

"THE GREAT ESCAPE" from THE CASAGRANDES SPECIAL "WE'RE ALL FAMILIA"
Derek Fridolfs — Writer
Suzannah Rowntree — Penciler
Zazo Aguiar — Inker, Colorist
Wilson Ramos Jr. — Letterer

TODD OMAN— Cover Artist

WACK

JORDAN ROSATO — Endpapers
JAMES SALERNO — Sr. Art Director/Nickelodeon
JAYJAY JACKSON — Design
EMMA BONE, CAITLIN FEIN, KRISTEN G. SMITH, NEIL WADE, DANA CLUVERIUS, MOLLIE FREILICH — Special Thanks
JEFF WHITMAN — Editor
JOAN HILTY — Editor/Nickelodeon
JIM SALICRUP
Editor-in-Chief

ISBN: 978-1-5458-0621-0 paperback edition
ISBN: 978-1-5458-0620-3 hardcover edition

www.papercutz.com

Papercutz books may be purchased for business or promotional use. For information on bulk purchases please contact Macmillan Corporate and Premium Sales Department at (800) 221-7945 x5442.

Printed in China
March 2021

Distributed by Macmillan
First Printing

MEET THE LOUD FAMILY and friends!

LINCOLN LOUD
THE MIDDLE CHILD

Lincoln is the middle child, with five older sisters and five younger sisters. He has learned that surviving the Loud household means staying a step ahead. He's the man with a plan, always coming up with a way to get what he wants or deal with a problem, even if things inevitably go wrong. Being the only boy comes with some perks. Lincoln gets his own room – even if it's just a converted linen closet. On the other hand, being the only boy also means he sometimes gets a little too much attention from his sisters. They mother him, tease him, and use him as the occasional lab rat or fashion show participant. Lincoln's sisters may drive him crazy, but he loves them and is always willing to help out if they need him.

LORI LOUD
THE OLDEST

As the first-born child of the Loud Clan, Lori sees herself as the boss of all her siblings. She feels she's paved the way for them and deserves extra respect. Her signature traits are rolling her eyes, texting her boyfriend, Bobby, and literally saying "literally" all the time. Because she's the oldest and most experienced sibling, Lori can be a great ally, so it pays to stay on her good side, especially since she can drive.

LENI LOUD
THE FASHIONISTA

Leni spends most of her time designing outfits and accessorizing. She always falls for Luan's pranks, and sometimes walks into walls when she's talking (she's not great at doing two things at once). Leni might be flighty, but she's the sweetest of the Loud siblings and truly has a heart of gold (even though she's pretty sure it's a heart of blood).

LUNA LOUD
THE ROCK STAR

Luna is loud, boisterous, freewheeling, and her energy is always cranked to 11. She thinks about music so much that she even talks in song lyrics. On the off-chance she doesn't have her guitar with her, everything can and will be turned into a musical instrument. You can always count on Luna to help out, and she'll do most anything you ask, as long as you're okay with her supplying a rocking guitar accompaniment.

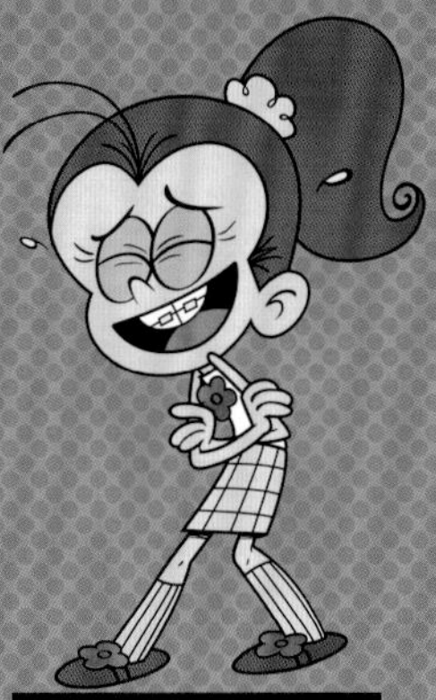

LUAN LOUD
THE JOKESTER

Luan's a standup comedienne who provides a nonstop barrage of silly puns. She's big on prop comedy too – squirting flowers and whoopee cushions – so you have to be on your toes whenever she's around. She loves to pull pranks and is a really good ventriloquist – she is often found doing bits with her dummy, Mr. Coconuts. Luan never lets anything get her down; to her, laughter IS the best medicine.

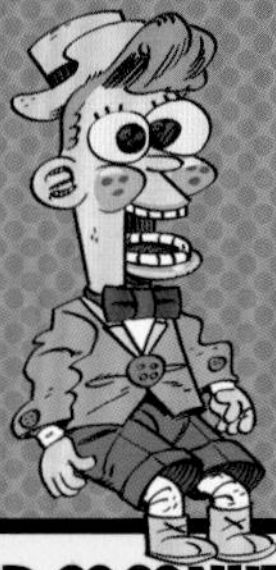

MR COCONUTS

Luan Loud's wise-cracking dummy.

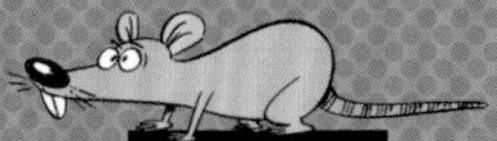

BITEY

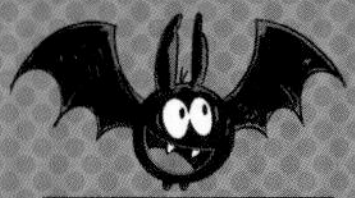

FANGS

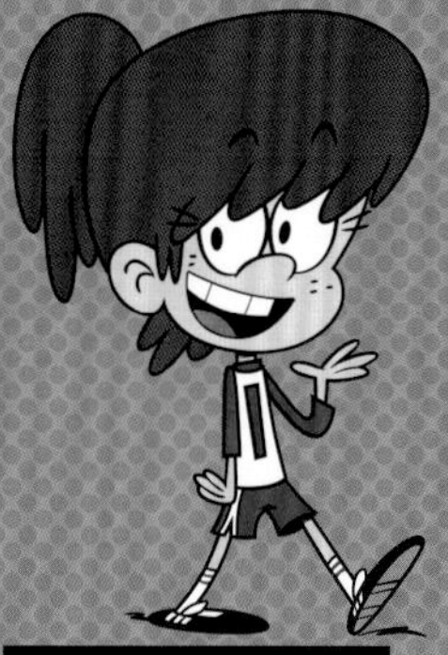

LYNN LOUD
THE ATHLETE

Lynn is athletic and full of energy and is always looking for a teammate. With her, it's all sports all the time. She'll turn anything into a sport. Putting away eggs? Jump shot! Score! Cleaning up the eggs? Slap shot! Score! Lynn is very competitive, but despite her competitive nature, she always tries to just have a good time.

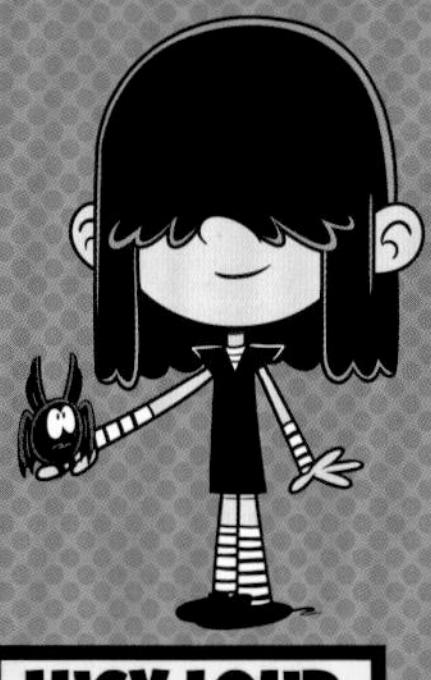

LUCY LOUD
THE EMO

You can always count on Lucy to give the morbid point of view in any given situation. She is obsessed with all things spooky and dark – funerals, vampires, séances, and the like. She wears mostly black and writes moody poetry. She's usually quiet and keeps to herself. Lucy has a way of mysteriously appearing out of nowhere, and try as they might, her siblings never get used to this.

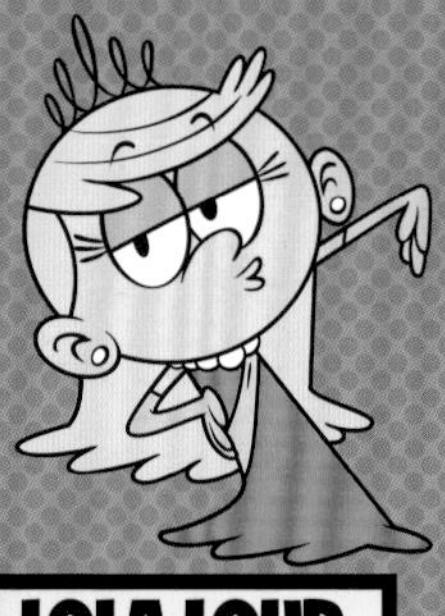

LOLA LOUD
THE BEAUTY QUEEN)

Lola could not be more different from her twin sister, Lana. She's a pageant powerhouse whose interests include glitter, photo shoots, and her own beautiful, beautiful face. But don't let her cute, gap-toothed smile fool you; underneath all the sugar and spice lurks a Machiavellian mastermind. Whatever Lola wants, Lola gets – or else. She's the eyes and ears of the household and never resists an opportunity to tattle on troublemakers. But if you stay on Lola's good side, you've got yourself a fierce ally – and a lifetime supply of free makeovers.

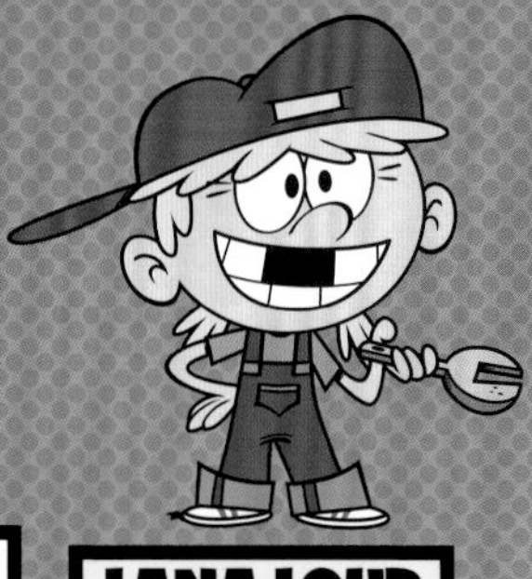

LANA LOUD
THE TOMBOY

Lana is the rough-and-tumble sparkplug counterpart to her twin sister, Lola. She's all about reptiles, mud pies, and muffler repair. She's the resident Ms. Fix-it and is always ready to lend a hand – the dirtier the job, the better. Need your toilet unclogged? Snake fed? Back-zit popped? Lana's your gal. All she asks in return is a little A-B-C gum, or a handful of kibble (she often sneaks it from the dog bowl).

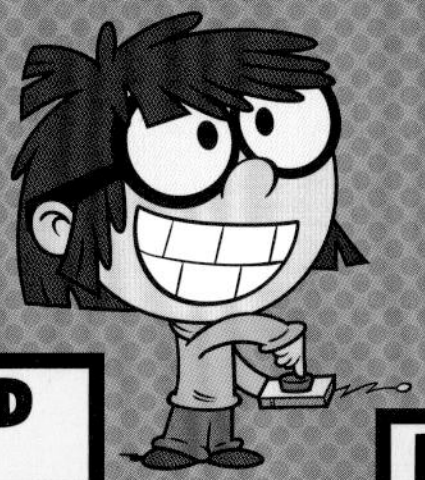

LISA LOUD
THE GENIUS

Lisa is smarter than the rest of her siblings combined. She'll most likely be a rocket scientist, or a brain surgeon, or an evil genius who takes over the world. Lisa spends most of her time working in her lab (the family has gotten used to the explosions), and says her research leaves little time for frivolous human pursuits like "playing" or "getting haircuts." That said, she's always there to help with a homework question, or to explain why the sky is blue, or to point out the structural flaws in someone's pillow fort. Lisa says it's the least she can do for her favorite test subjects, er, siblings.

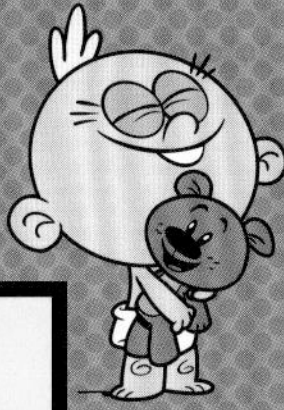

LILY LOUD
THE BABY

Lily is a giggly, drooly, diaper-ditching free spirit, affectionately known as "the poop machine." You can't keep a nappy on this kid – she's like a teething Houdini. But even when Lily's running wild, dropping rancid diaper bombs, or drooling all over the remote, she always brings a smile to everyone's face (and a clothespin to their nose). Lily is everyone's favorite little buddy, and the whole family loves her unconditionally.

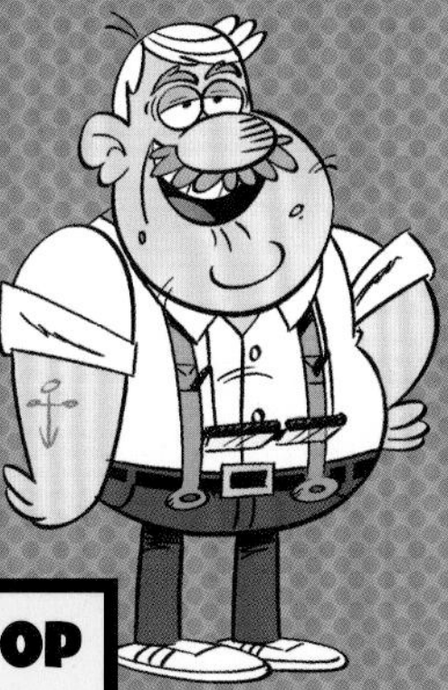

POP POP

Albert, the Loud kids' grandfather, currently lives at Sunset Canyon Retirement Community after dedicating his life to working in the military. Pop Pop spends his days dominating at shuffleboard, eating pudding, and going on adventures with his pals Bernie, Scoots, and Seymour and his girlfriend, Myrtle. Pop Pop is upbeat, fun-loving, and cherishes spending time with his grandchildren.

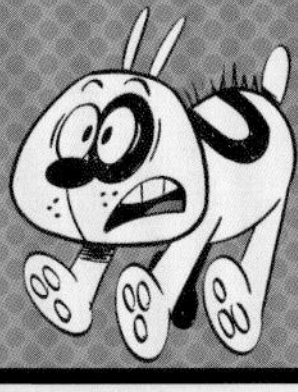

CHARLES

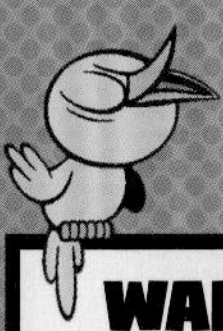

WALT

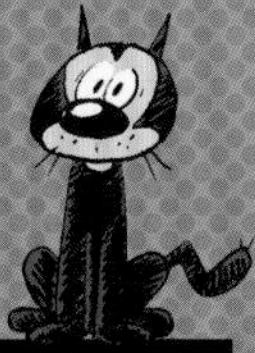

CLIFF

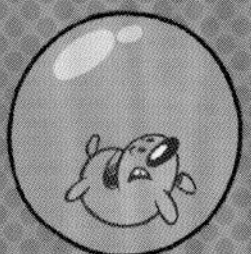

GEO

RITA LOUD

Mother to the eleven Loud kids, Mom (Rita Loud) wears many different hats. She's a chauffeur, homework-checker, and barf-cleaner-upper all rolled into one. She's always there for her kids and ready to jump into action during a crisis, whether it's a fight between the twins or Leni's missing shoe. When she's not chasing the kids around or at her day job as a dental hygienist, Mom pursues her passion: writing. She also loves taking on house projects and is very handy with tools (guess that's where Lana gets it from). Between writing, working, and being a mom, her days are always hectic but she wouldn't have it any other way.

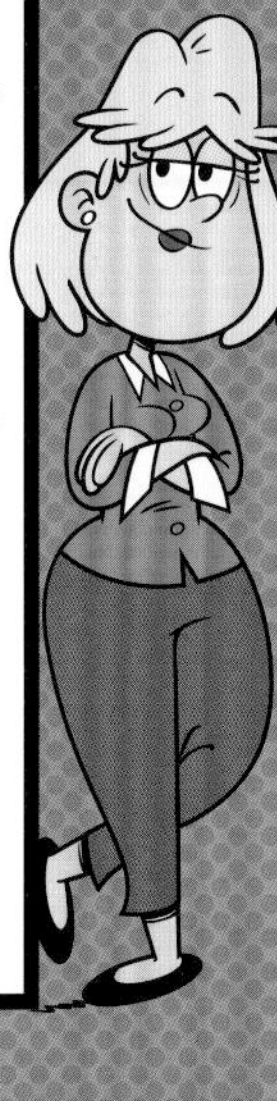

LYNN LOUD SR.

Dad (Lynn Loud Sr.) is a fun-loving, upbeat aspiring chef. A kid-at-heart, he's not above taking part in the kids' zany schemes. In addition to cooking, Dad loves his van, playing the cowbell. and making puns. Before meeting Mom, Dad spent a semester in England and has been obsessed with British culture ever since – and sometimes "accidentally" slips into a British accent. When Dad's not wrangling the kids, he's pursuing his dream of opening his own restaurant where he hopes to make his "Lynn-sagnas" world-famous.

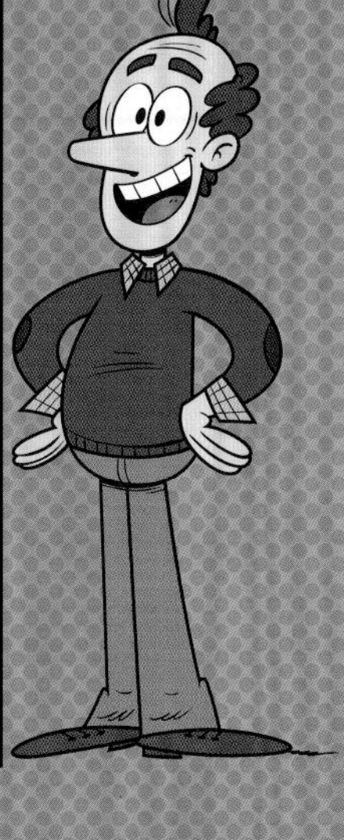

CLYDE McBRIDE
THE BEST FRIEND

Clyde is Lincoln's partner in crime. He's always willing to go along with Lincoln's crazy schemes (even if he sees the flaws in them up-front). Lincoln and Clyde are two peas in a pod and share pretty much all of the same tastes in movies, comics, TV shows, toys — you name it. As an only child, Clyde envies Lincoln — how cool would it be to always have siblings around to talk to? But since Clyde spends so much time at the Loud household, he's almost an honorary sibling anyway.

ZACH GURDLE

Zach is a self-admitted nerd who's obsessed with aliens and conspiracy theories. He lives between a freeway and a circus, so the chaos of the Loud House doesn't faze him. He and Rusty occasionally butt heads, but deep down, it's all love.

RUSTY SPOKES

Rusty is a self-proclaimed ladies' man who's always the first to dish out girl advice — even though he's never been on an actual date. His dad owns a suit rental service, so occasionally Rusty can hook the gang up with some dapper duds — just as long as no one gets anything dirty.

LIAM

Liam is an enthusiastic, sweet-natured farm boy full of down-home wisdom. He loves hanging out with his Mee Maw, wrestling his prize pig Virginia, and sharing his farm-to-table produce with the rest of the gang.

STELLA

Stella Zhau is a quirky, carefree girl who's new to Royal Woods. She has tons of interests, like trying on wigs, playing laser tag, eating curly fries, and hanging with her friends. But what she loves the most is tech — she always wants to dismantle electronics and put them back together again.

MR. BUD GROUSE

Mr. Grouse is the Louds's next-door-neighbor. The Louds often go to him for favors which he normally rejects – unless there's a chance for him to score one of Dad's famous Lynn-sagnas. Mr. Grouse loves gardening, relaxing in his recliner, and keeping anything of the Louds's that flies into his yard (his catchphrase, after all, is "my yard, my property!").

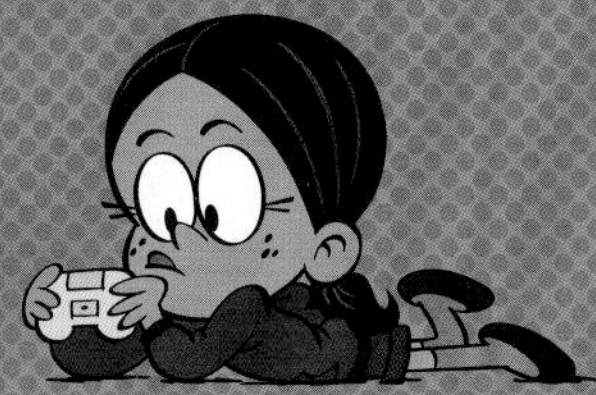

RONNIE ANNE SANTIAGO

Ronnie Anne's a skateboarding city girl now. She's fearless, free-spirited, and always quick to come up with a plan. She's one tough cookie, but she also has a sweet side. Ronnie Anne loves helping her family, and that's taught her to help others, too. When she's not pitching in at the family mercado, you can find her exploring the neighborhood with her best friend Sid, or ordering hot dogs with her skater buds Casey, Nikki, and Sameer.

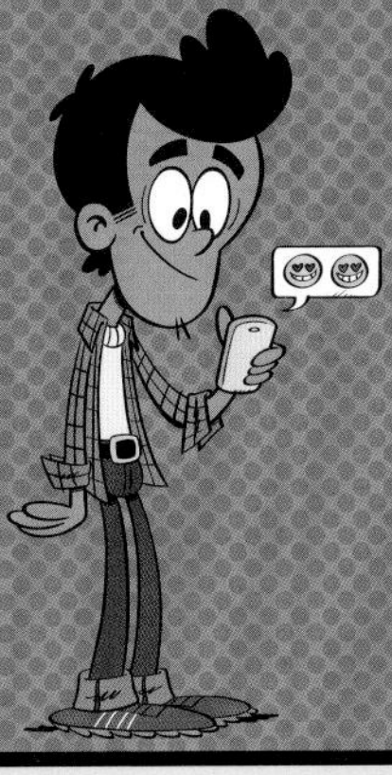

BOBBY SANTIAGO

Bobby is Ronnie Anne's big bro. He's a student and one of the hardest workers in the city! He loves his family and loves working at the Mercado. As his Abuelo's right hand man, Bobby can't wait to take over the family business one day. He's a big kid at heart, and his clumsiness gets him into some sticky situations at work, like locking himself in the freezer. Mercado mishaps aside, everyone in the neighborhood loves to come to the store and talk to Bobby.

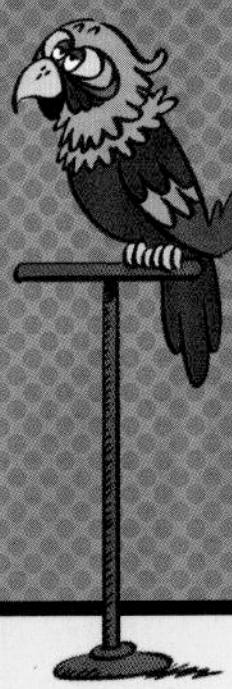

SERGIO

Sergio is the Casagrandes' beloved pet parrot. He's a blunt, sassy bird who "thinks" he's full of wisdom, and always has something to say. The Casagrandes have to keep a close eye on their credit card as Sergio is addicted to online shopping and is always asking the family to buy him some new gadget he saw on TV. Sergio is most loyal to Rosa and serves as her wing-man, partner in crime, taste tester, and confidant. Sergio is quite popular in the neighborhood and is always up for a good time.

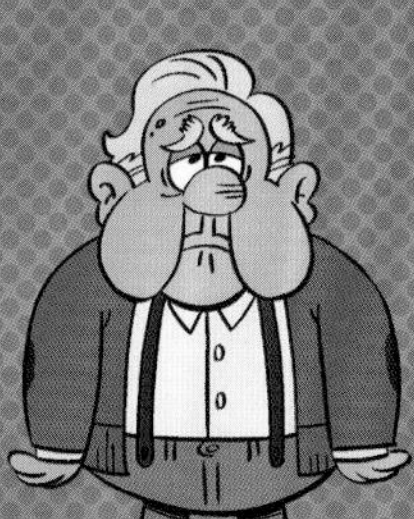

VITO FILLIPONIO

Vito is one of Rosa and Hector's oldest and dearest friends, and a frequent customer at the Mercado. He's lovable, nosy, and usually overstays his welcome, but there is nothing he wouldn't do for his loved ones and his dogs, Big Tony and Little Sal.

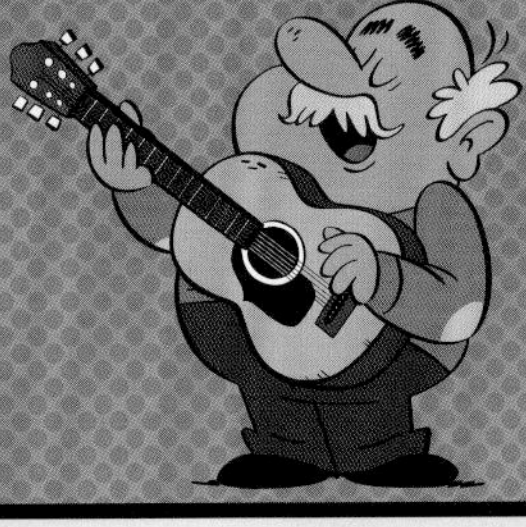

HECTOR CASAGRANDE

Hector is Carlos and Maria's dad, and the Abuelo of the family (that means grandpa)! He owns the Mercado on the ground floor of their apartment building and takes great pride in his work, his family, and being the unofficial "mayor" of the block. He loves to tell stories, share his ideas, and gossip (even though he won't admit to it). You can find him working in the Mercado, playing guitar, or watching his favorite telenovela.

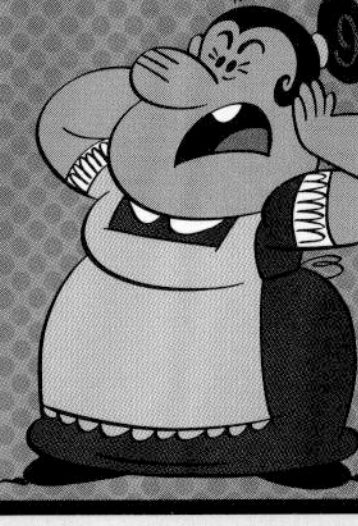

ROSA CASAGRANDE

Rosa is Carlos and Maria's mom and the Abuela of the family (that means grandma)! She's the head of the household, the wisest Casagrande, and the master cook with a superhuman ability to tell when anyone in the house is hungry. She often tries to fix problems or illnesses with traditional Mexican home remedies and potions. She's very protective of her family... sometimes a little too much.

"THE CASE OF THE STOLEN DRAWERS"

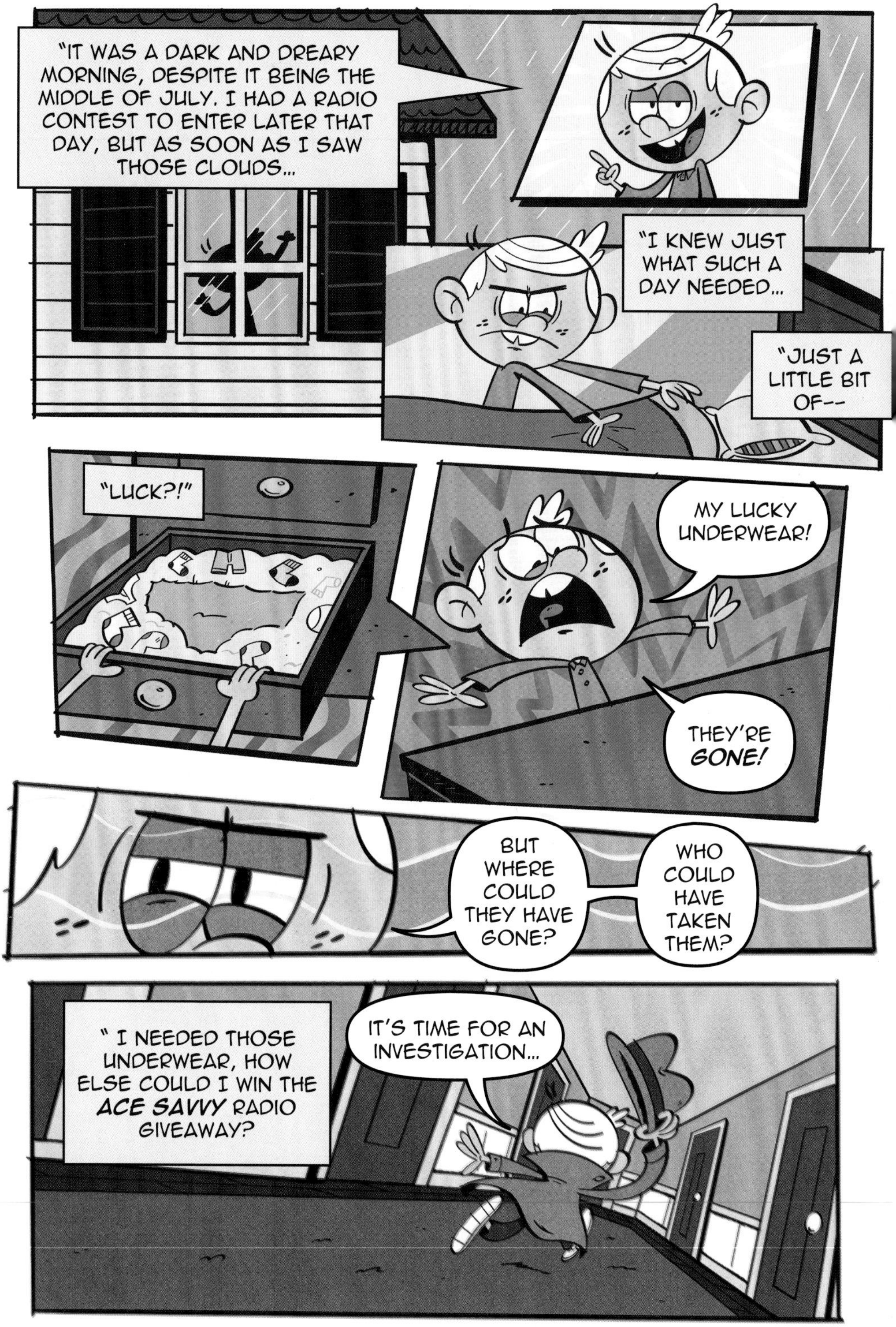
"IT WAS A DARK AND DREARY MORNING, DESPITE IT BEING THE MIDDLE OF JULY. I HAD A RADIO CONTEST TO ENTER LATER THAT DAY, BUT AS SOON AS I SAW THOSE CLOUDS...
"I KNEW JUST WHAT SUCH A DAY NEEDED...
"JUST A LITTLE BIT OF--
"LUCK?!"
MY LUCKY UNDERWEAR!
THEY'RE *GONE!*
BUT WHERE COULD THEY HAVE GONE?
WHO COULD HAVE TAKEN THEM?
" I NEEDED THOSE UNDERWEAR, HOW ELSE COULD I WIN THE *ACE SAVVY* RADIO GIVEAWAY?
IT'S TIME FOR AN INVESTIGATION...

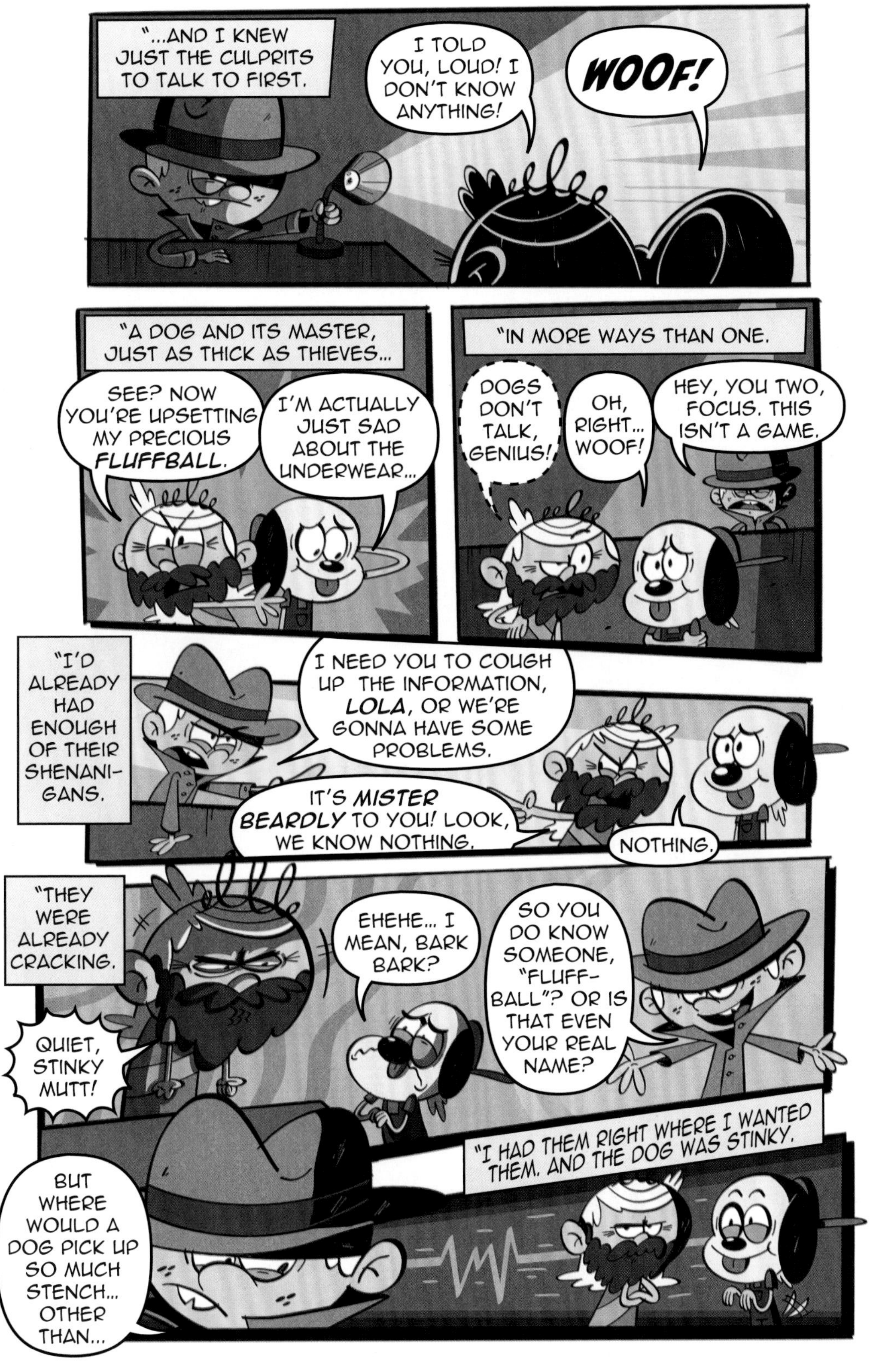
"...AND I KNEW JUST THE CULPRITS TO TALK TO FIRST.
I TOLD YOU, LOUD! I DON'T KNOW ANYTHING!
WOOF!
"A DOG AND ITS MASTER, JUST AS THICK AS THIEVES...
SEE? NOW YOU'RE UPSETTING MY PRECIOUS FLUFFBALL.
I'M ACTUALLY JUST SAD ABOUT THE UNDERWEAR...
"IN MORE WAYS THAN ONE.
DOGS DON'T TALK, GENIUS!
OH, RIGHT... WOOF!
HEY, YOU TWO, FOCUS. THIS ISN'T A GAME.
"I'D ALREADY HAD ENOUGH OF THEIR SHENANI-GANS.
I NEED YOU TO COUGH UP THE INFORMATION, LOLA, OR WE'RE GONNA HAVE SOME PROBLEMS.
IT'S MISTER BEARDLY TO YOU! LOOK, WE KNOW NOTHING.
NOTHING.
"THEY WERE ALREADY CRACKING.
EHEHE... I MEAN, BARK BARK?
SO YOU DO KNOW SOMEONE, "FLUFF-BALL"? OR IS THAT EVEN YOUR REAL NAME?
QUIET, STINKY MUTT!
"I HAD THEM RIGHT WHERE I WANTED THEM. AND THE DOG WAS STINKY.
BUT WHERE WOULD A DOG PICK UP SO MUCH STENCH... OTHER THAN...

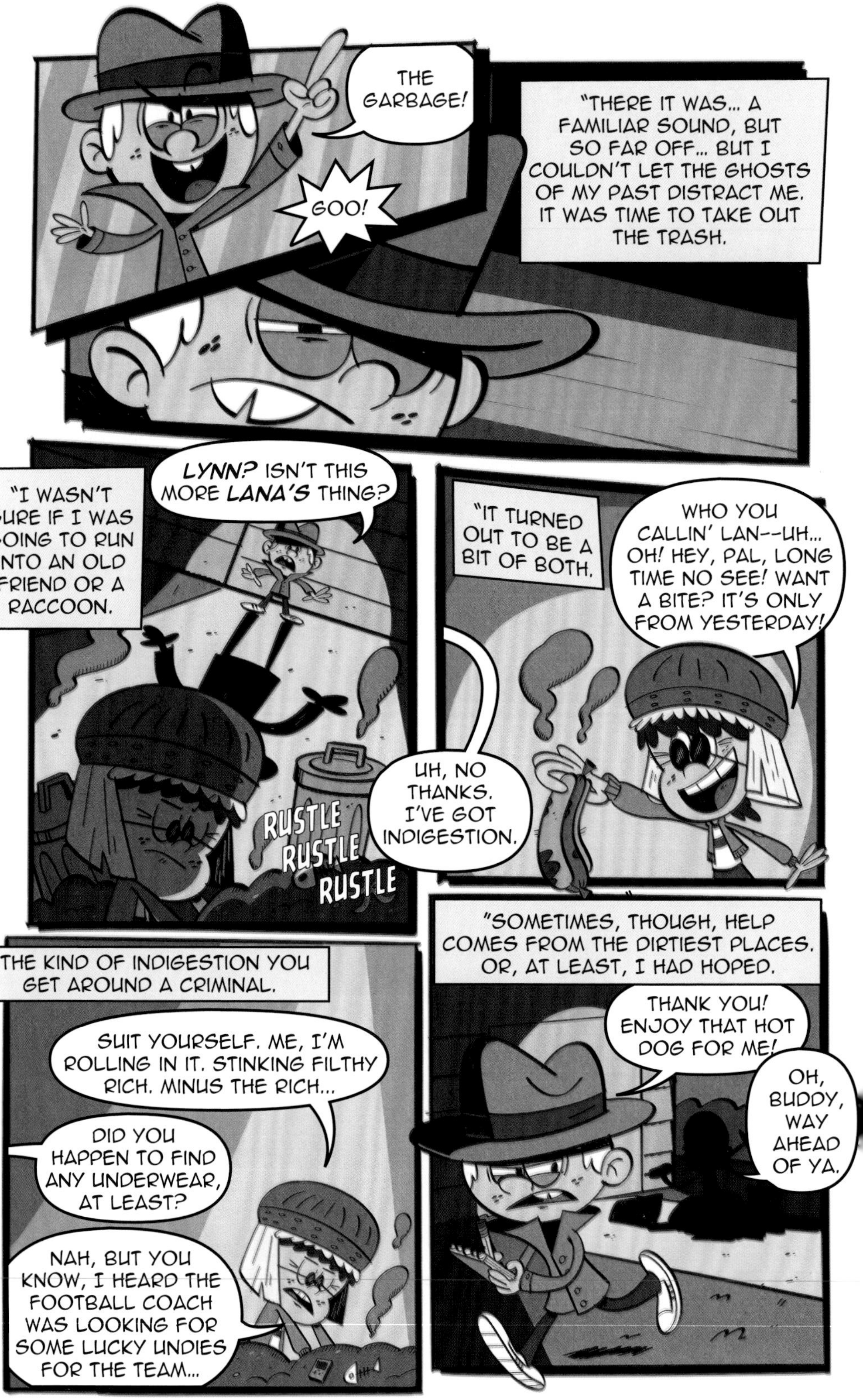
THE GARBAGE!
GOO!
"THERE IT WAS... A FAMILIAR SOUND, BUT SO FAR OFF... BUT I COULDN'T LET THE GHOSTS OF MY PAST DISTRACT ME. IT WAS TIME TO TAKE OUT THE TRASH.
"I WASN'T SURE IF I WAS GOING TO RUN INTO AN OLD FRIEND OR A RACCOON.
LYNN? ISN'T THIS MORE LANA'S THING?
RUSTLE RUSTLE RUSTLE
"IT TURNED OUT TO BE A BIT OF BOTH.
WHO YOU CALLIN' LAN--UH... OH! HEY, PAL, LONG TIME NO SEE! WANT A BITE? IT'S ONLY FROM YESTERDAY!
UH, NO THANKS. I'VE GOT INDIGESTION.
"THE KIND OF INDIGESTION YOU GET AROUND A CRIMINAL.
SUIT YOURSELF. ME, I'M ROLLING IN IT. STINKING FILTHY RICH. MINUS THE RICH...
DID YOU HAPPEN TO FIND ANY UNDERWEAR, AT LEAST?
NAH, BUT YOU KNOW, I HEARD THE FOOTBALL COACH WAS LOOKING FOR SOME LUCKY UNDIES FOR THE TEAM...
"SOMETIMES, THOUGH, HELP COMES FROM THE DIRTIEST PLACES. OR, AT LEAST, I HAD HOPED.
THANK YOU! ENJOY THAT HOT DOG FOR ME!
OH, BUDDY, WAY AHEAD OF YA.

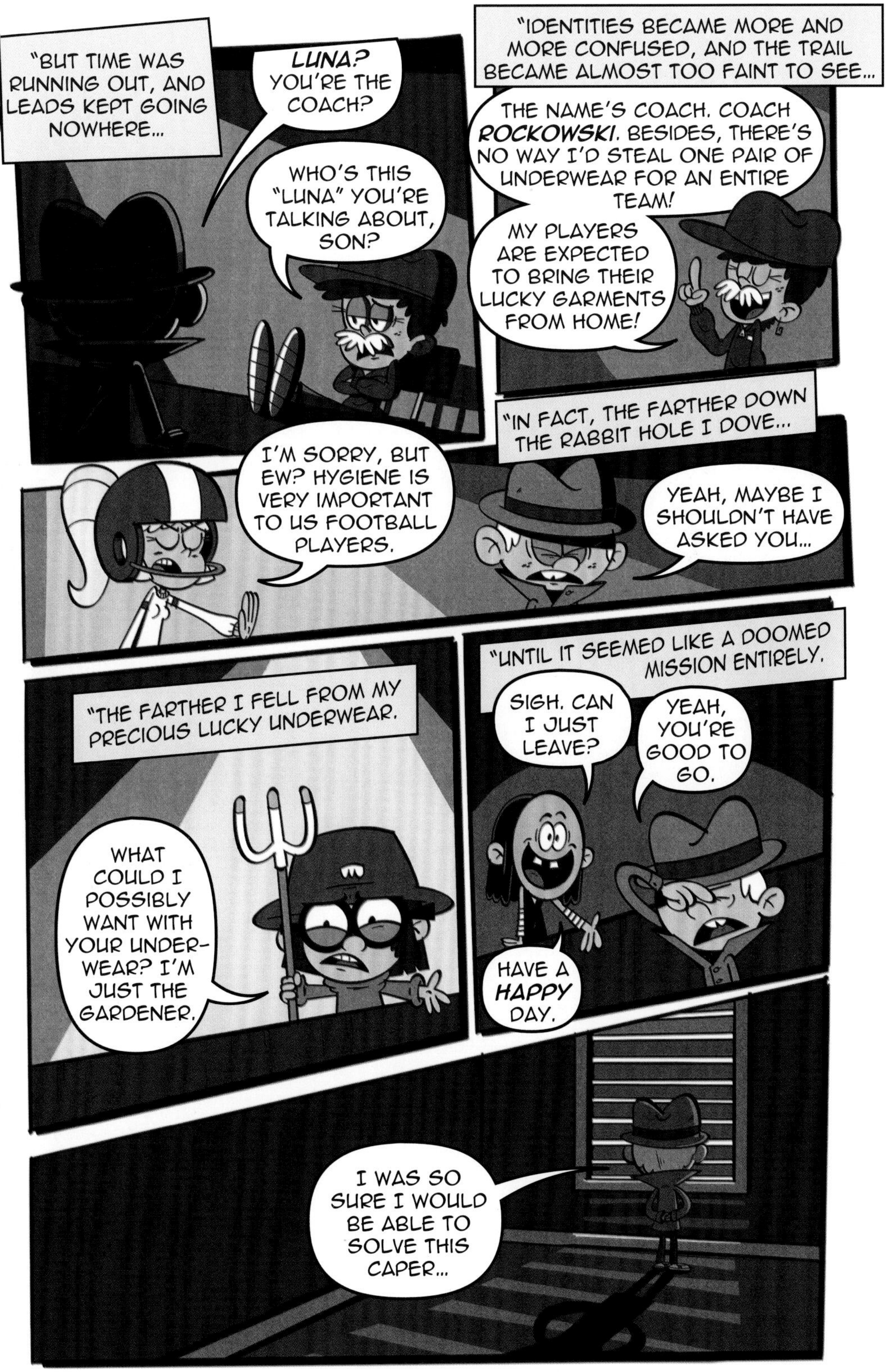

"BUT TIME WAS RUNNING OUT, AND LEADS KEPT GOING NOWHERE...
LUNA? YOU'RE THE COACH?
WHO'S THIS "LUNA" YOU'RE TALKING ABOUT, SON?
"IDENTITIES BECAME MORE AND MORE CONFUSED, AND THE TRAIL BECAME ALMOST TOO FAINT TO SEE...
THE NAME'S COACH. COACH ROCKOWSKI. BESIDES, THERE'S NO WAY I'D STEAL ONE PAIR OF UNDERWEAR FOR AN ENTIRE TEAM!
MY PLAYERS ARE EXPECTED TO BRING THEIR LUCKY GARMENTS FROM HOME!
"IN FACT, THE FARTHER DOWN THE RABBIT HOLE I DOVE...
I'M SORRY, BUT EW? HYGIENE IS VERY IMPORTANT TO US FOOTBALL PLAYERS.
YEAH, MAYBE I SHOULDN'T HAVE ASKED YOU...
"THE FARTHER I FELL FROM MY PRECIOUS LUCKY UNDERWEAR.
WHAT COULD I POSSIBLY WANT WITH YOUR UNDER-WEAR? I'M JUST THE GARDENER.
"UNTIL IT SEEMED LIKE A DOOMED MISSION ENTIRELY.
SIGH. CAN I JUST LEAVE?
YEAH, YOU'RE GOOD TO GO.
HAVE A HAPPY DAY.
I WAS SO SURE I WOULD BE ABLE TO SOLVE THIS CAPER...

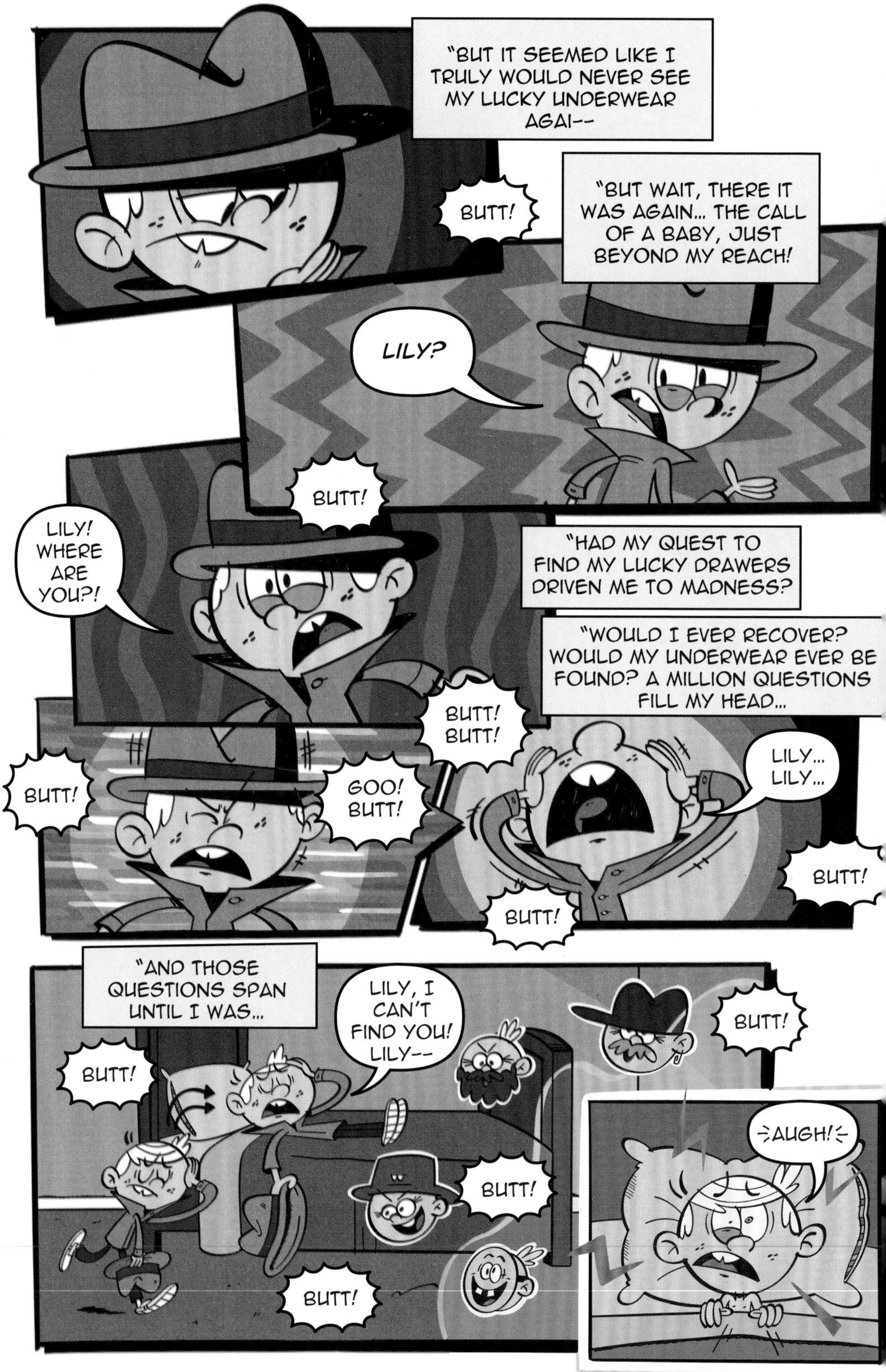
"BUT IT SEEMED LIKE I TRULY WOULD NEVER SEE MY LUCKY UNDERWEAR AGAI--
BUTT!
"BUT WAIT, THERE IT WAS AGAIN... THE CALL OF A BABY, JUST BEYOND MY REACH!
LILY?
BUTT!
LILY! WHERE ARE YOU?!
"HAD MY QUEST TO FIND MY LUCKY DRAWERS DRIVEN ME TO MADNESS?
"WOULD I EVER RECOVER? WOULD MY UNDERWEAR EVER BE FOUND? A MILLION QUESTIONS FILL MY HEAD...
BUTT! BUTT!
BUTT!
GOO! BUTT!
LILY... LILY...
BUTT!
BUTT!
"AND THOSE QUESTIONS SPAN UNTIL I WAS...
LILY, I CAN'T FIND YOU! LILY--
BUTT!
BUTT!
BUTT!
BUTT!
AUGH!

LILY? I JUST HAD THE WEIRDEST DREAM... I THOUGHT I LOST MY--

--MY LUCKY UNDERWEAR!

COME ON, COME ON, WHERE ARE THEY?

BUTT!

OH...WHAT? I COMPLETELY FORGOT, I MUST HAVE GONE TO SLEEP IN THESE AND FORGOTTEN... THANKS, LILY.

BUT WAIT...

LILY, YOU'RE MISSING YOUR DIAPER! YOU KNOW WHAT THAT MEANS...

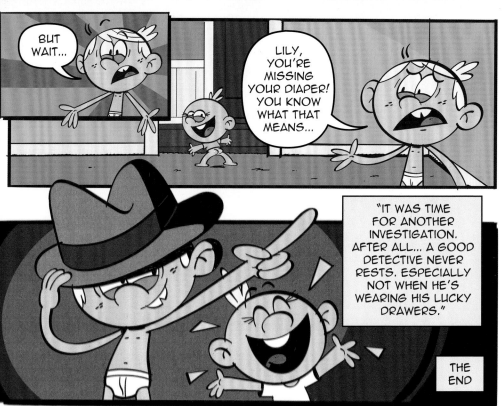

"IT WAS TIME FOR ANOTHER INVESTIGATION. AFTER ALL... A GOOD DETECTIVE NEVER RESTS. ESPECIALLY NOT WHEN HE'S WEARING HIS LUCKY DRAWERS."

THE END

"GOING COCO-NUTS!"

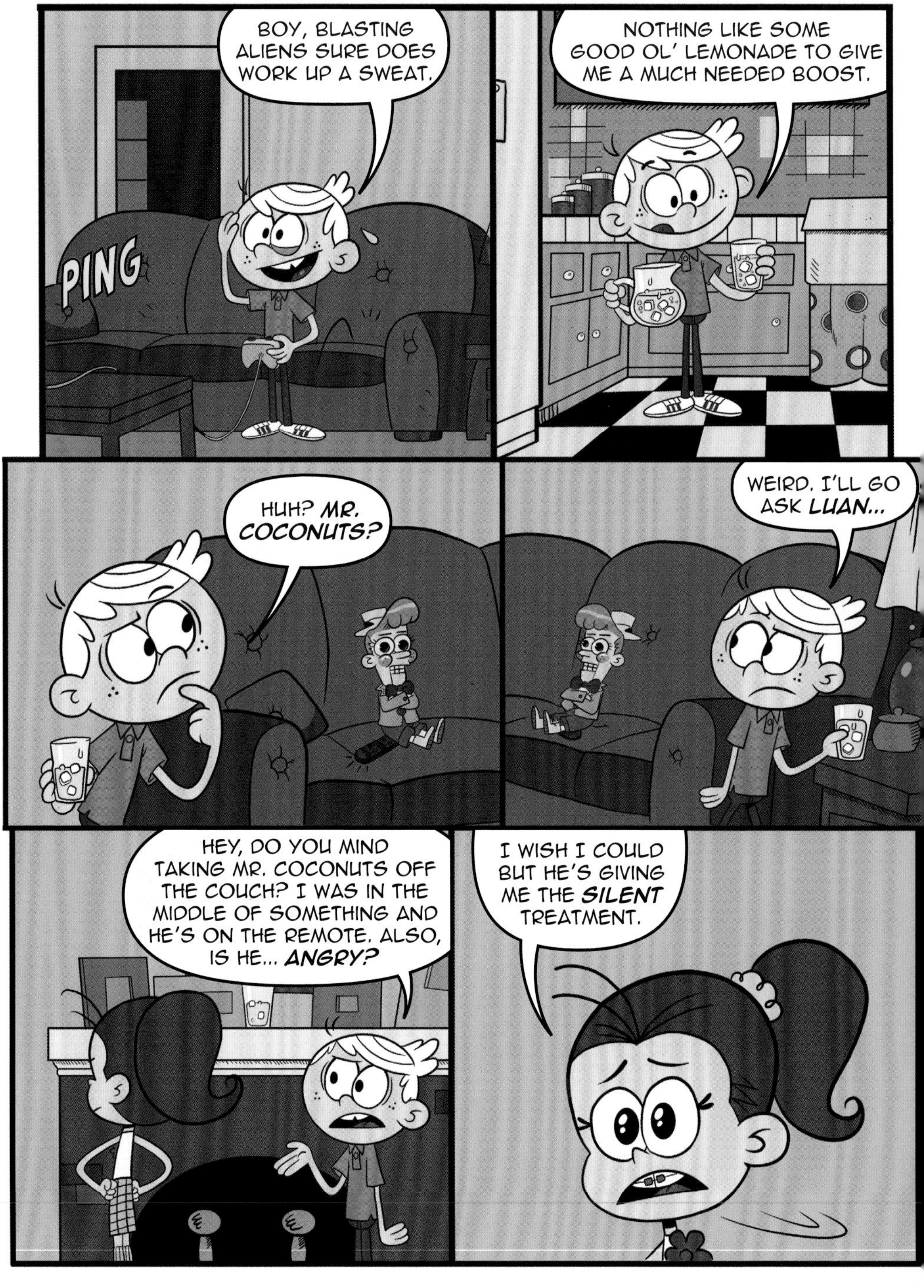
BOY, BLASTING ALIENS SURE DOES WORK UP A SWEAT.
PING
NOTHING LIKE SOME GOOD OL' LEMONADE TO GIVE ME A MUCH NEEDED BOOST.
HUH? MR. COCONUTS?
WEIRD. I'LL GO ASK LUAN...
HEY, DO YOU MIND TAKING MR. COCONUTS OFF THE COUCH? I WAS IN THE MIDDLE OF SOMETHING AND HE'S ON THE REMOTE. ALSO, IS HE... ANGRY?
I WISH I COULD BUT HE'S GIVING ME THE SILENT TREATMENT.

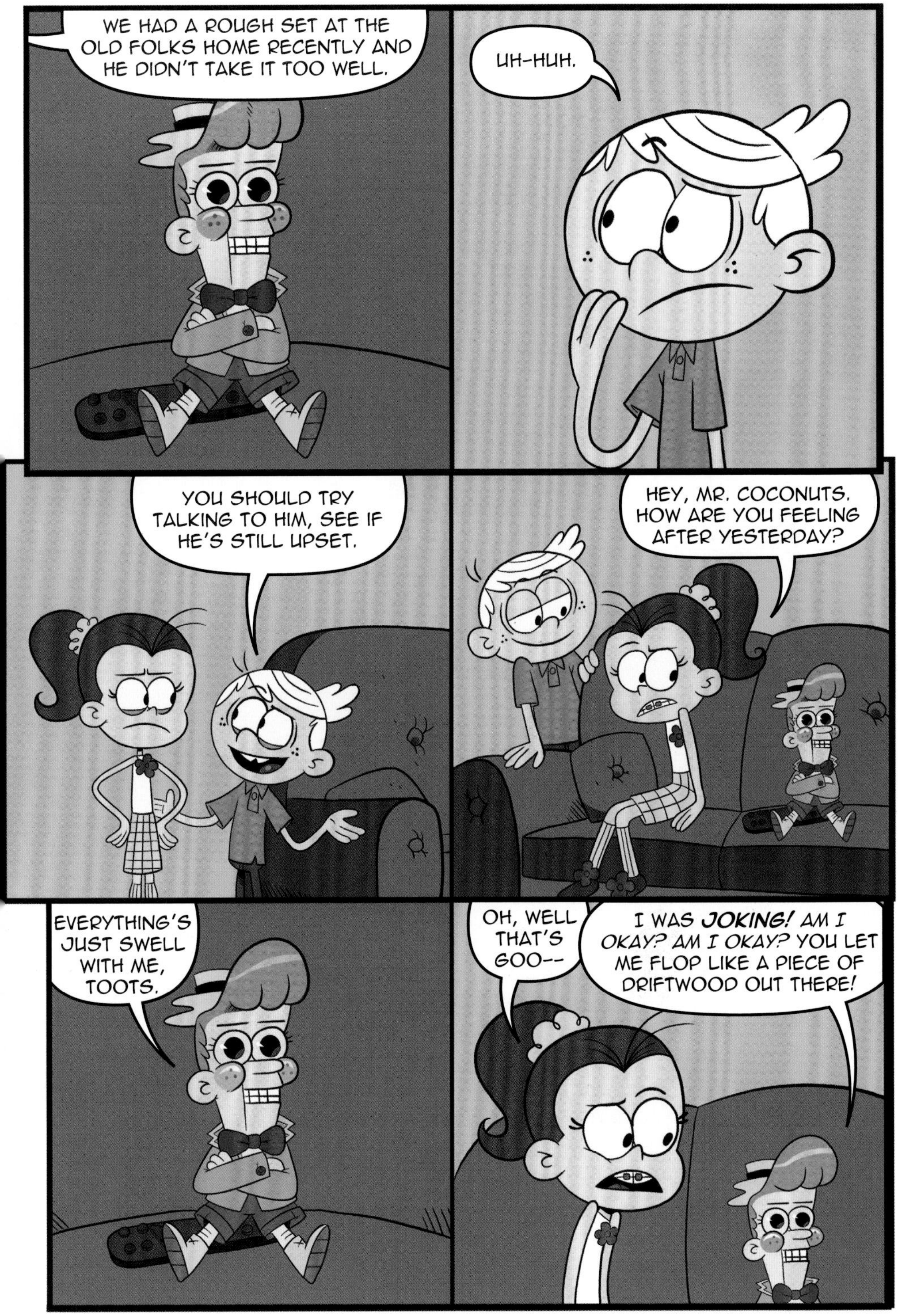
WE HAD A ROUGH SET AT THE OLD FOLKS HOME RECENTLY AND HE DIDN'T TAKE IT TOO WELL.
UH-HUH.
YOU SHOULD TRY TALKING TO HIM, SEE IF HE'S STILL UPSET.
HEY, MR. COCONUTS. HOW ARE YOU FEELING AFTER YESTERDAY?
EVERYTHING'S JUST SWELL WITH ME, TOOTS.
OH, WELL THAT'S GOO--
I WAS ***JOKING!*** *AM I OKAY? AM I OKAY?* YOU LET ME FLOP LIKE A PIECE OF DRIFTWOOD OUT THERE!

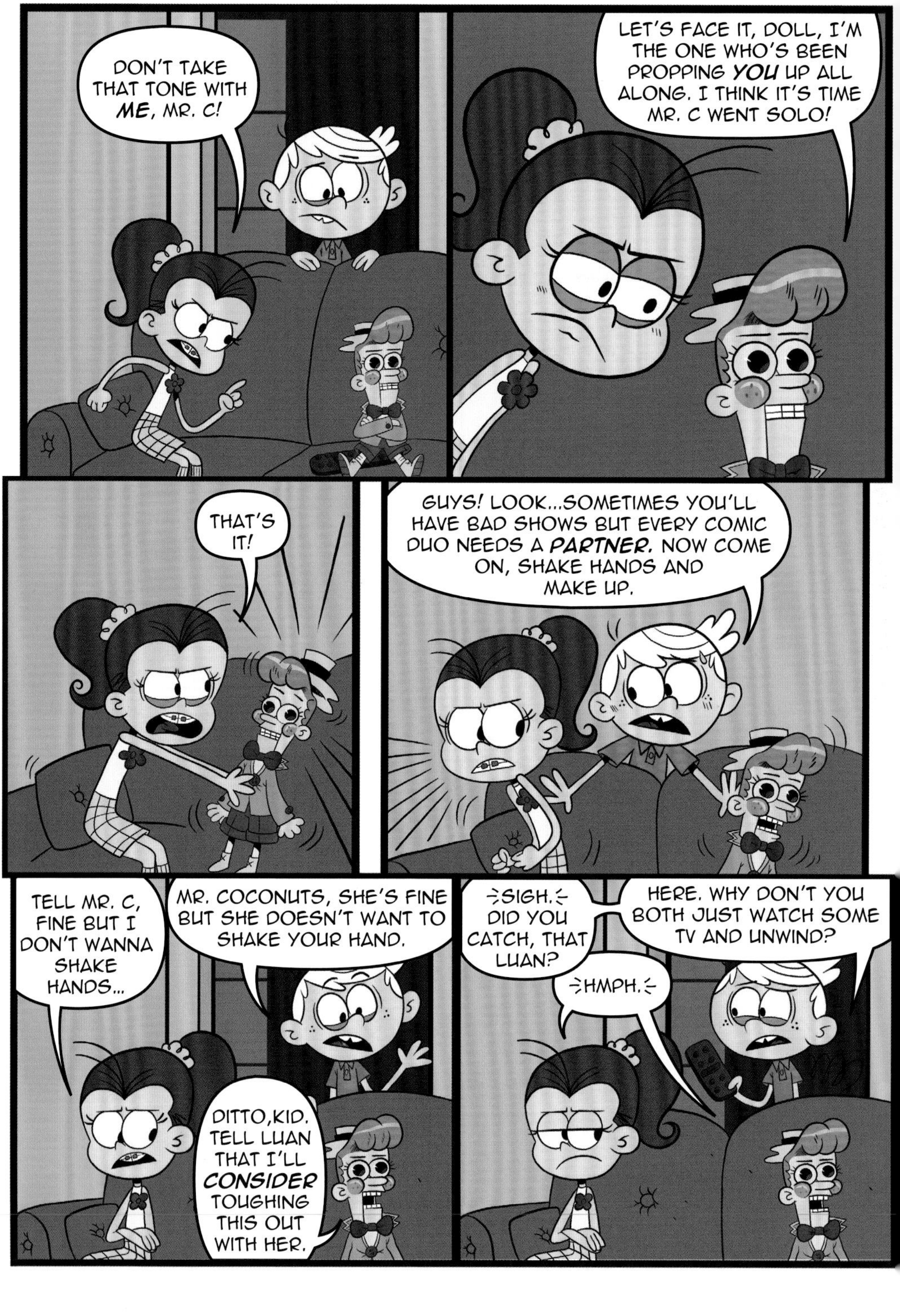
DON'T TAKE THAT TONE WITH *ME*, MR. C!
LET'S FACE IT, DOLL, I'M THE ONE WHO'S BEEN PROPPING *YOU* UP ALL ALONG. I THINK IT'S TIME MR. C WENT SOLO!
THAT'S IT!
GUYS! LOOK...SOMETIMES YOU'LL HAVE BAD SHOWS BUT EVERY COMIC DUO NEEDS A *PARTNER.* NOW COME ON, SHAKE HANDS AND MAKE UP.
TELL MR. C, FINE BUT I DON'T WANNA SHAKE HANDS...
MR. COCONUTS, SHE'S FINE BUT SHE DOESN'T WANT TO SHAKE YOUR HAND.
DITTO,KID. TELL LUAN THAT I'LL *CONSIDER* TOUGHING THIS OUT WITH HER.
SIGH.
DID YOU CATCH, THAT LUAN?
HMPH.
HERE. WHY DON'T YOU BOTH JUST WATCH SOME TV AND UNWIND?

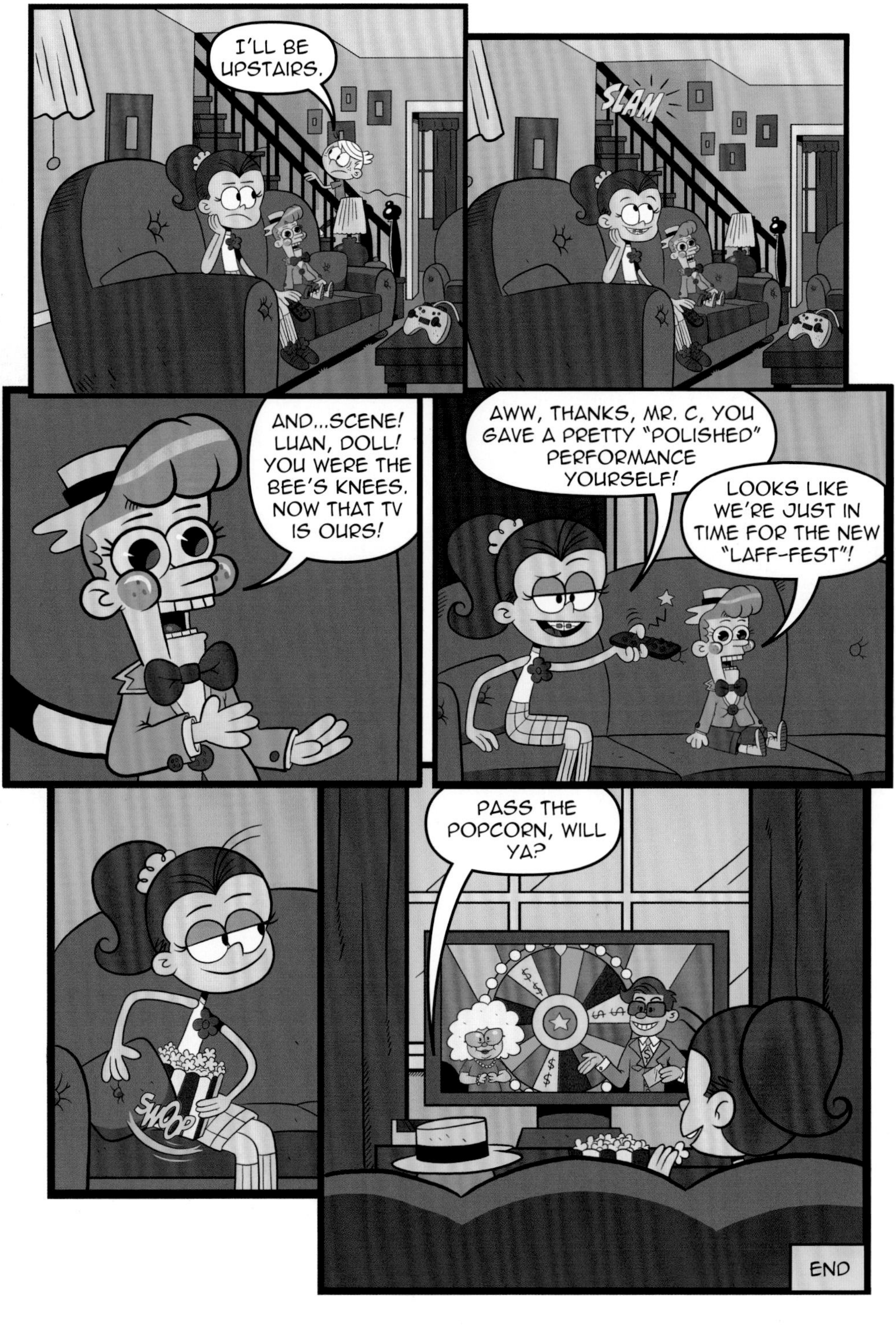
I'LL BE UPSTAIRS.
SLAM
AND...SCENE! LUAN, DOLL! YOU WERE THE BEE'S KNEES. NOW THAT TV IS OURS!
AWW, THANKS, MR. C, YOU GAVE A PRETTY "POLISHED" PERFORMANCE YOURSELF!
LOOKS LIKE WE'RE JUST IN TIME FOR THE NEW "LAFF-FEST"!
SWOOP
PASS THE POPCORN, WILL YA?
END

"OLLIE OLLIE OXEN FREE"

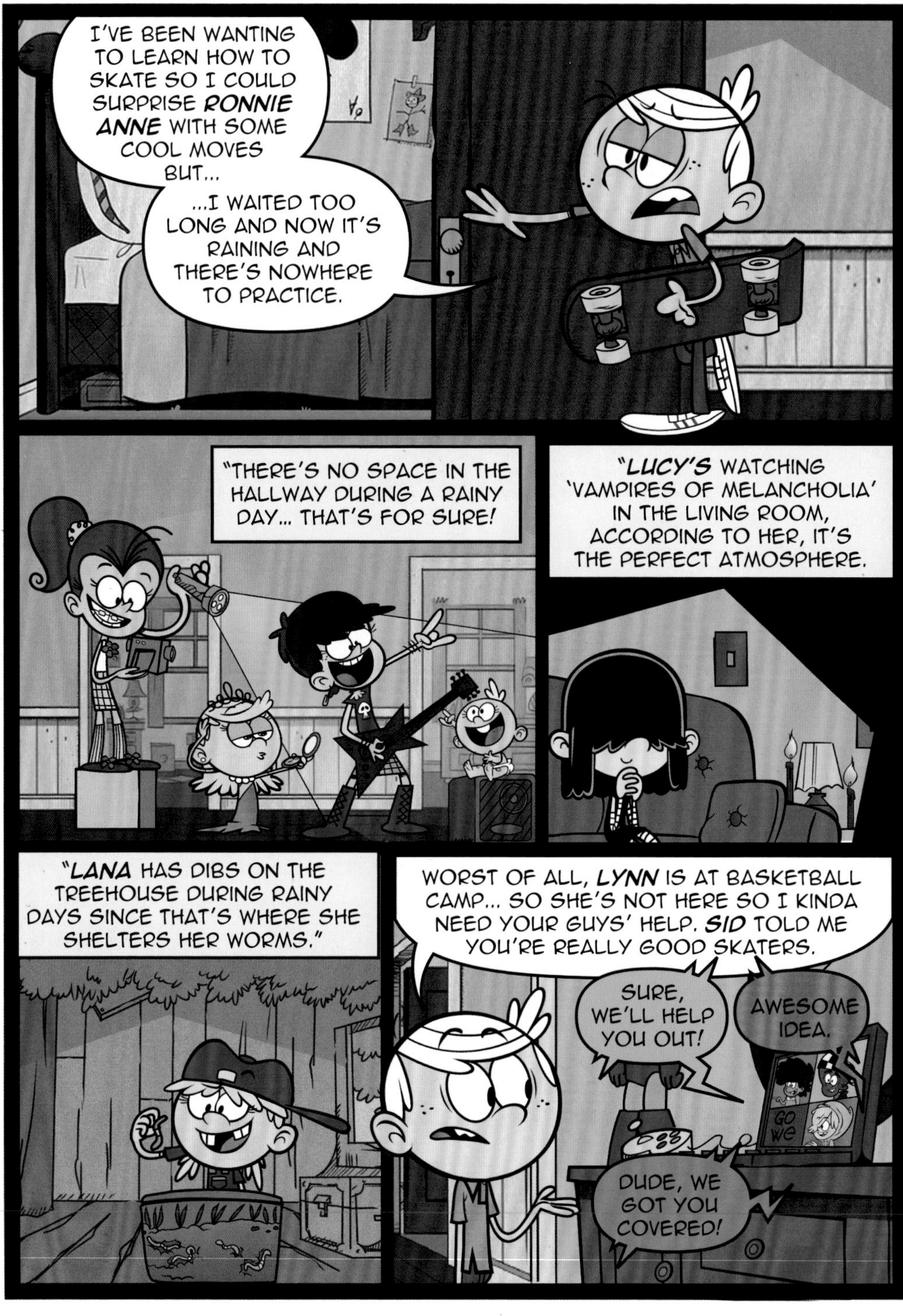
I'VE BEEN WANTING TO LEARN HOW TO SKATE SO I COULD SURPRISE RONNIE ANNE WITH SOME COOL MOVES BUT...
...I WAITED TOO LONG AND NOW IT'S RAINING AND THERE'S NOWHERE TO PRACTICE.
"THERE'S NO SPACE IN THE HALLWAY DURING A RAINY DAY... THAT'S FOR SURE!
"LUCY'S WATCHING 'VAMPIRES OF MELANCHOLIA' IN THE LIVING ROOM, ACCORDING TO HER, IT'S THE PERFECT ATMOSPHERE.
"LANA HAS DIBS ON THE TREEHOUSE DURING RAINY DAYS SINCE THAT'S WHERE SHE SHELTERS HER WORMS."
WORST OF ALL, LYNN IS AT BASKETBALL CAMP... SO SHE'S NOT HERE SO I KINDA NEED YOUR GUYS' HELP. SID TOLD ME YOU'RE REALLY GOOD SKATERS.
SURE, WE'LL HELP YOU OUT!
AWESOME IDEA.
DUDE, WE GOT YOU COVERED!

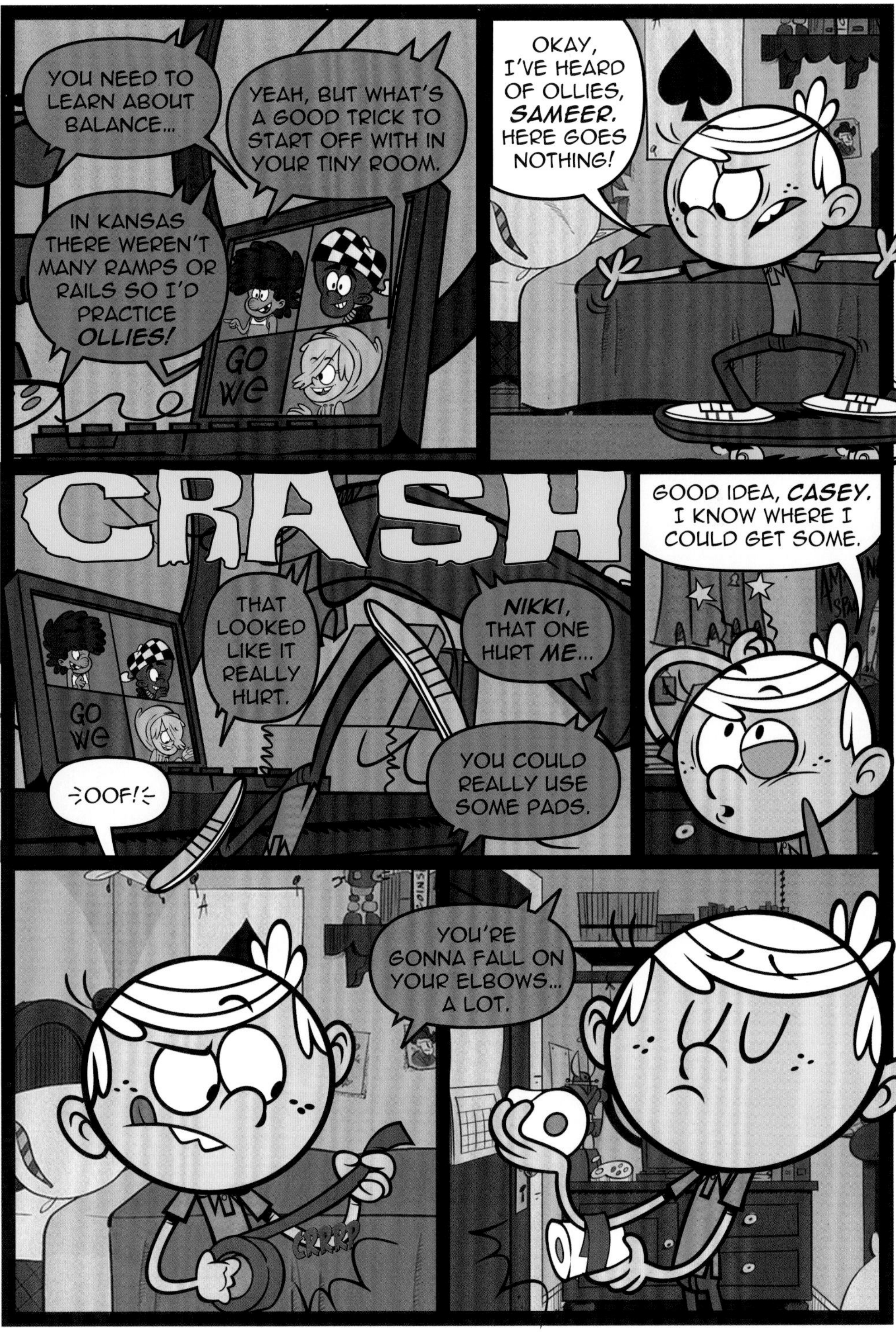
YOU NEED TO LEARN ABOUT BALANCE...
YEAH, BUT WHAT'S A GOOD TRICK TO START OFF WITH IN YOUR TINY ROOM.
IN KANSAS THERE WEREN'T MANY RAMPS OR RAILS SO I'D PRACTICE OLLIES!
GO WE
OKAY, I'VE HEARD OF OLLIES, SAMEER. HERE GOES NOTHING!
CRASH
GO WE
THAT LOOKED LIKE IT REALLY HURT.
NIKKI, THAT ONE HURT ME...
OOF!
YOU COULD REALLY USE SOME PADS.
GOOD IDEA, CASEY. I KNOW WHERE I COULD GET SOME.
YOU'RE GONNA FALL ON YOUR ELBOWS... A LOT.
CRRRP

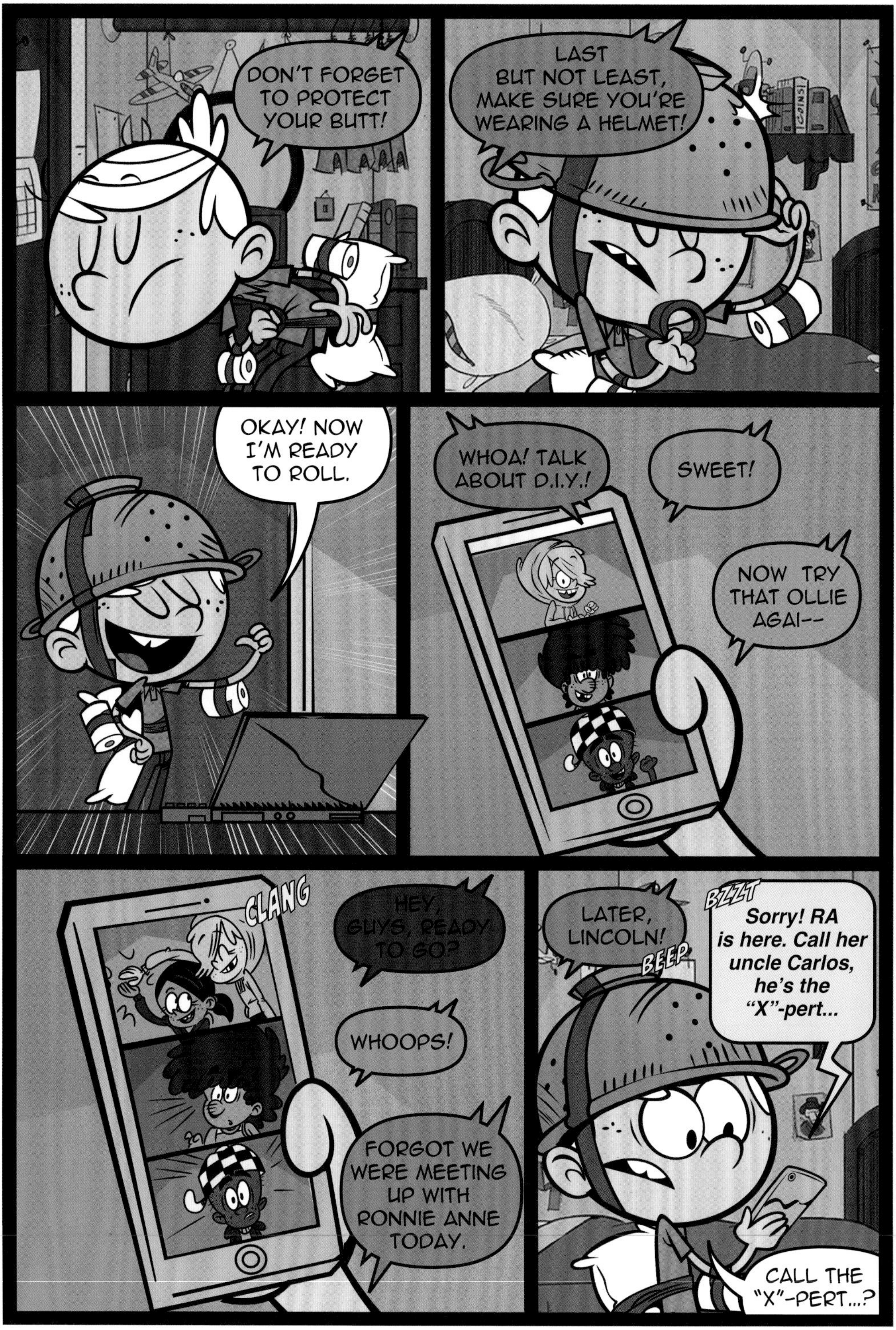
DON'T FORGET TO PROTECT YOUR BUTT!
LAST BUT NOT LEAST, MAKE SURE YOU'RE WEARING A HELMET!
OKAY! NOW I'M READY TO ROLL.
WHOA! TALK ABOUT D.I.Y.!
SWEET!
NOW TRY THAT OLLIE AGAI--
CLANG
HEY, GUYS, READY TO GO?
WHOOPS!
FORGOT WE WERE MEETING UP WITH RONNIE ANNE TODAY.
LATER, LINCOLN!
BEEP
BZZZT
Sorry! RA is here. Call her uncle Carlos, he's the "X"-pert...
CALL THE "X"-PERT...?

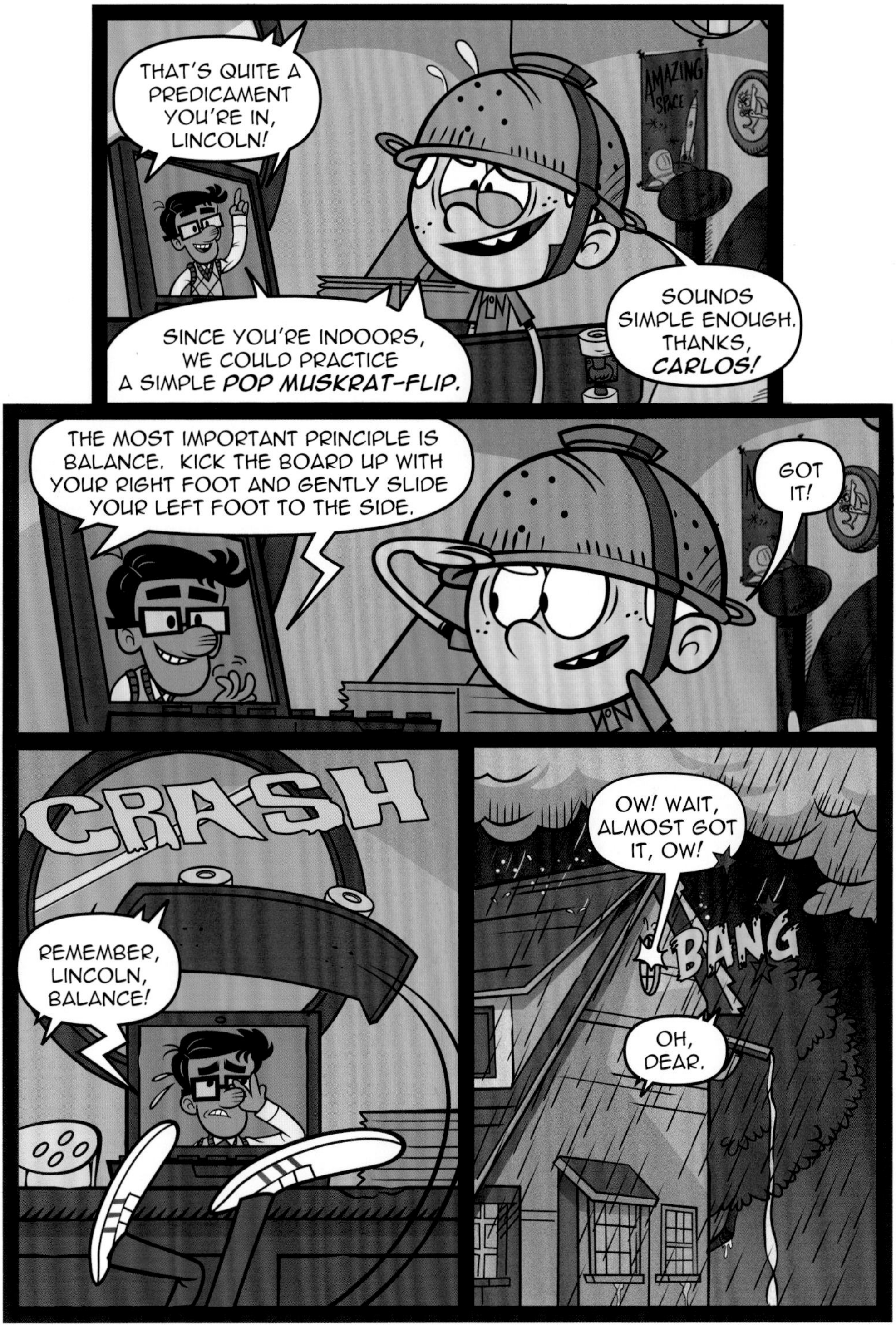
THAT'S QUITE A PREDICAMENT YOU'RE IN, LINCOLN!
SINCE YOU'RE INDOORS, WE COULD PRACTICE A SIMPLE POP MUSKRAT-FLIP.
SOUNDS SIMPLE ENOUGH. THANKS, CARLOS!
AMAZING SPACE
THE MOST IMPORTANT PRINCIPLE IS BALANCE. KICK THE BOARD UP WITH YOUR RIGHT FOOT AND GENTLY SLIDE YOUR LEFT FOOT TO THE SIDE.
GOT IT!
CRASH
REMEMBER, LINCOLN, BALANCE!
OW! WAIT, ALMOST GOT IT, OW!
BANG
OH, DEAR.

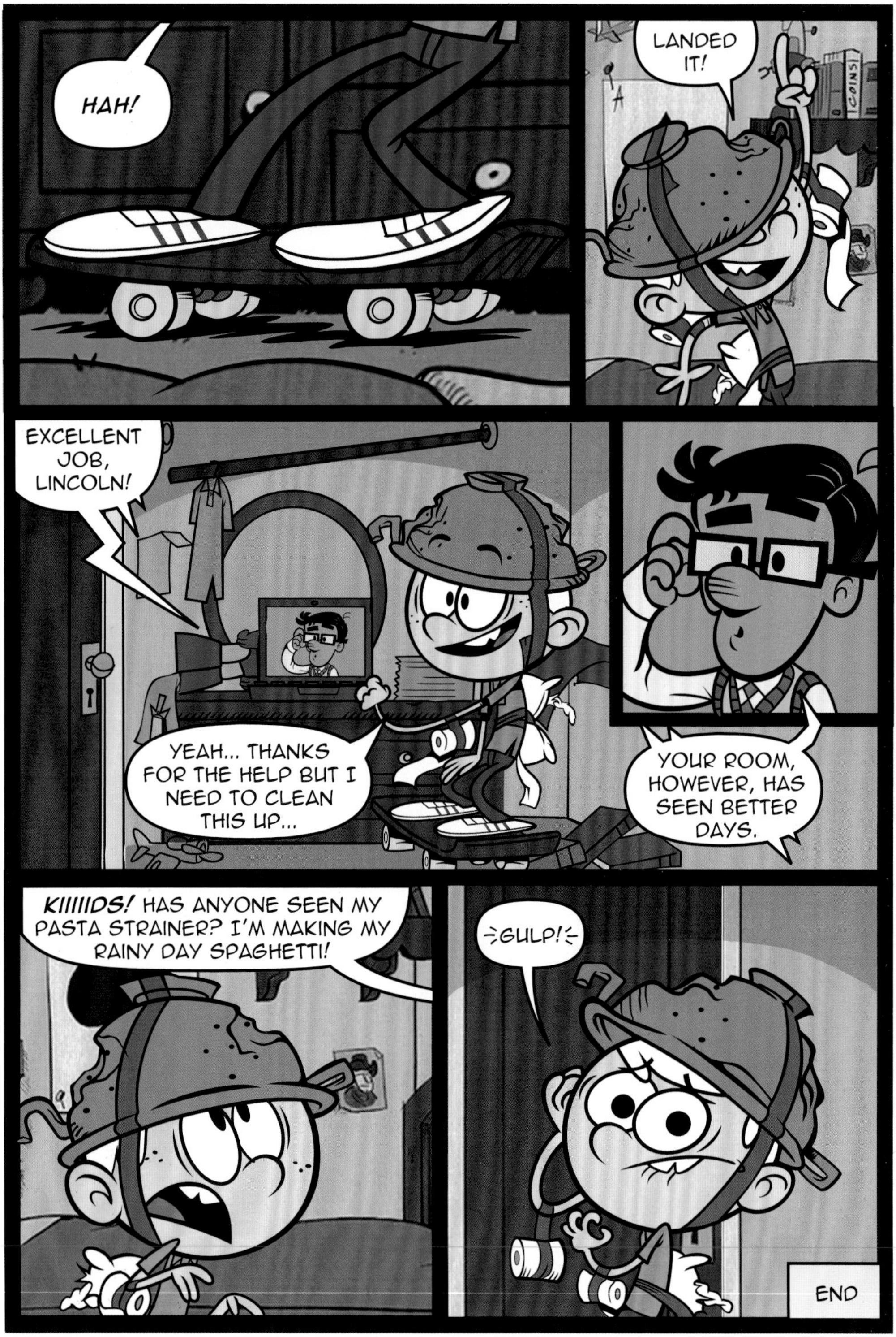
HAH!
LANDED IT!
EXCELLENT JOB, LINCOLN!
YEAH... THANKS FOR THE HELP BUT I NEED TO CLEAN THIS UP...
YOUR ROOM, HOWEVER, HAS SEEN BETTER DAYS.
KIIIIIDS! HAS ANYONE SEEN MY PASTA STRAINER? I'M MAKING MY RAINY DAY SPAGHETTI!
GULP!
END

"TONGUE-TIED"

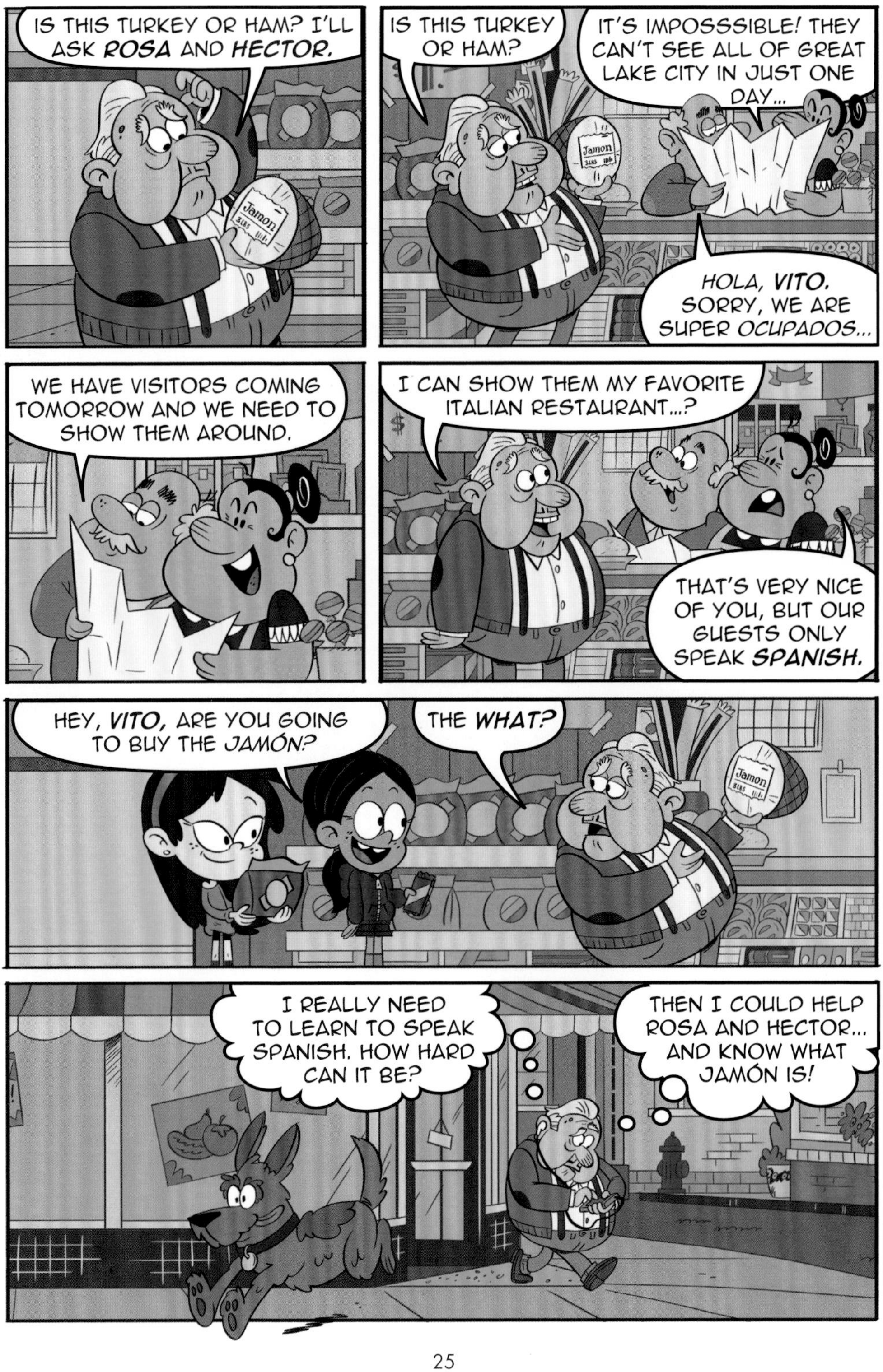
IS THIS TURKEY OR HAM? I'LL ASK ROSA AND HECTOR.
Jamon
IS THIS TURKEY OR HAM?
IT'S IMPOSSSIBLE! THEY CAN'T SEE ALL OF GREAT LAKE CITY IN JUST ONE DAY...
HOLA, VITO. SORRY, WE ARE SUPER OCUPADOS...
WE HAVE VISITORS COMING TOMORROW AND WE NEED TO SHOW THEM AROUND.
I CAN SHOW THEM MY FAVORITE ITALIAN RESTAURANT...?
THAT'S VERY NICE OF YOU, BUT OUR GUESTS ONLY SPEAK SPANISH.
HEY, VITO, ARE YOU GOING TO BUY THE JAMÓN?
THE WHAT?
I REALLY NEED TO LEARN TO SPEAK SPANISH. HOW HARD CAN IT BE?
THEN I COULD HELP ROSA AND HECTOR... AND KNOW WHAT JAMÓN IS!

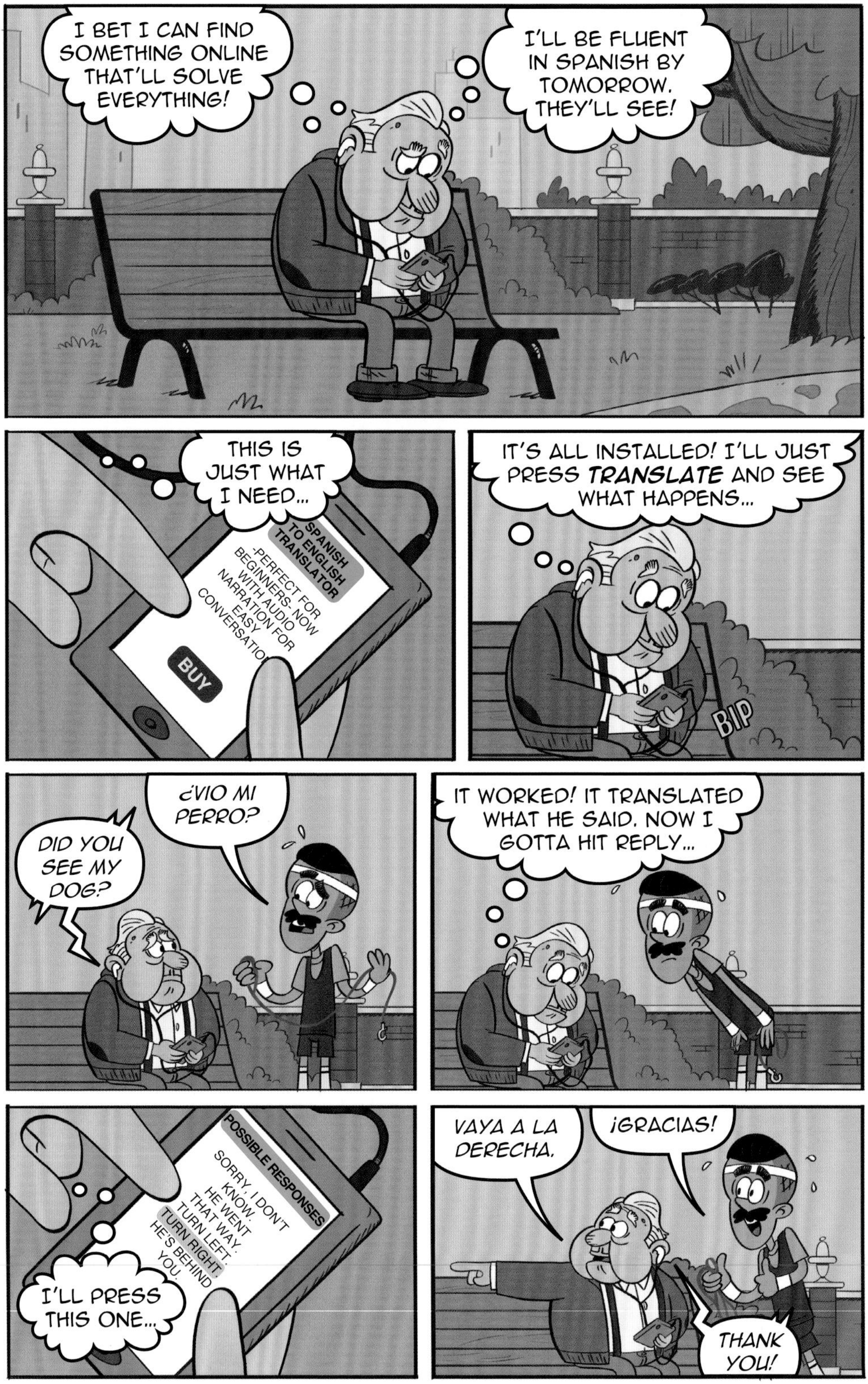
I BET I CAN FIND SOMETHING ONLINE THAT'LL SOLVE EVERYTHING!
I'LL BE FLUENT IN SPANISH BY TOMORROW. THEY'LL SEE!
THIS IS JUST WHAT I NEED...
SPANISH TO ENGLISH TRANSLATOR
-PERFECT FOR BEGINNERS. NOW WITH AUDIO NARRATION FOR EASY CONVERSATION
BUY
IT'S ALL INSTALLED! I'LL JUST PRESS TRANSLATE AND SEE WHAT HAPPENS...
BIP
¿VIO MI PERRO?
DID YOU SEE MY DOG?
IT WORKED! IT TRANSLATED WHAT HE SAID. NOW I GOTTA HIT REPLY...
POSSIBLE RESPONSES
SORRY, I DON'T KNOW.
HE WENT THAT WAY.
TURN LEFT.
TURN RIGHT.
HE'S BEHIND YOU.
I'LL PRESS THIS ONE...
VAYA A LA DERECHA.
¡GRACIAS!
THANK YOU!

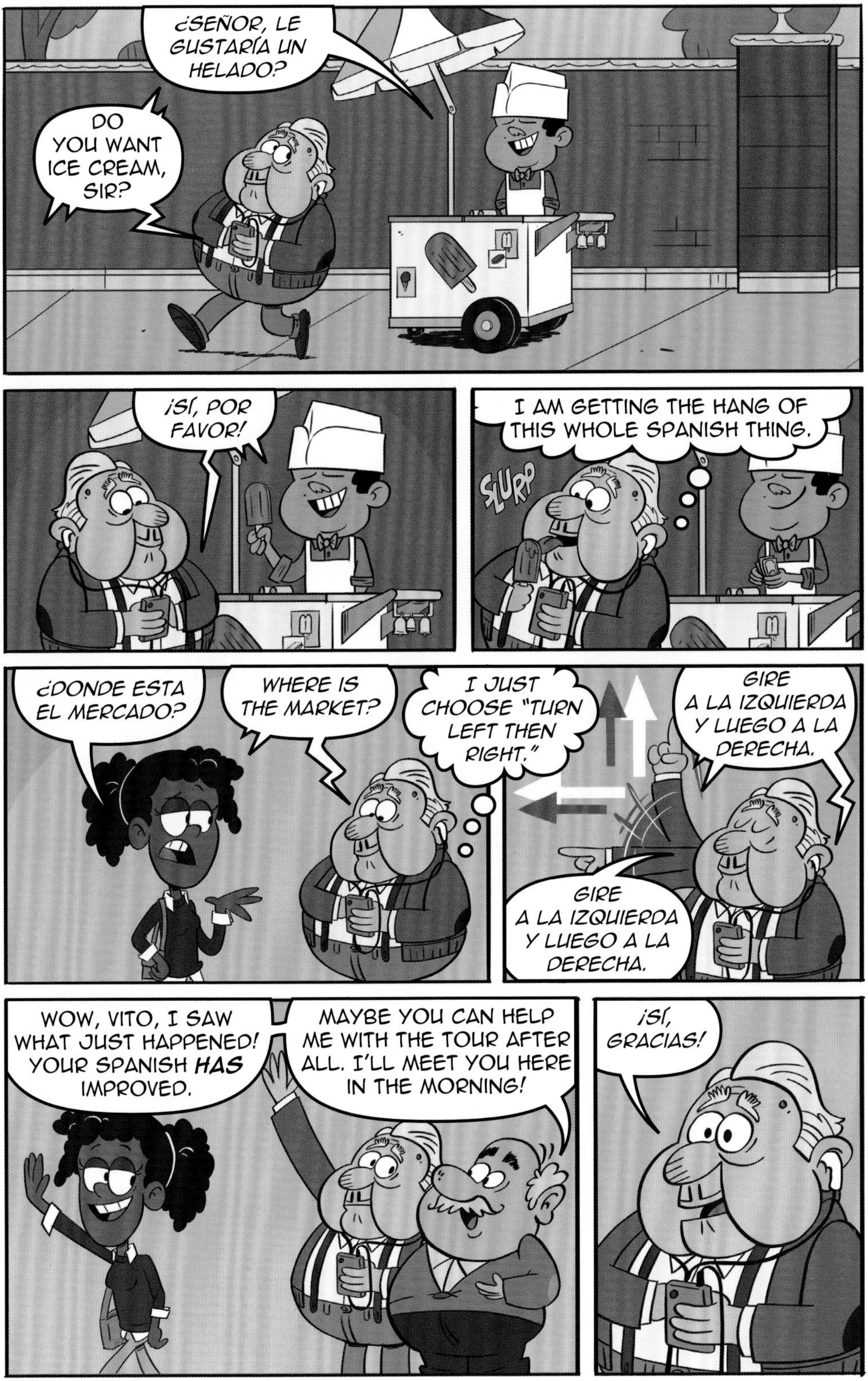
¿SEÑOR, LE GUSTARÍA UN HELADO?
DO YOU WANT ICE CREAM, SIR?
¡SÍ, POR FAVOR!
I AM GETTING THE HANG OF THIS WHOLE SPANISH THING.
SLURP
¿DONDE ESTA EL MERCADO?
WHERE IS THE MARKET?
I JUST CHOOSE "TURN LEFT THEN RIGHT."
GIRE A LA IZQUIERDA Y LUEGO A LA DERECHA.
GIRE A LA IZQUIERDA Y LUEGO A LA DERECHA.
WOW, VITO, I SAW WHAT JUST HAPPENED! YOUR SPANISH **HAS** IMPROVED.
MAYBE YOU CAN HELP ME WITH THE TOUR AFTER ALL. I'LL MEET YOU HERE IN THE MORNING!
¡SÍ, GRACIAS!

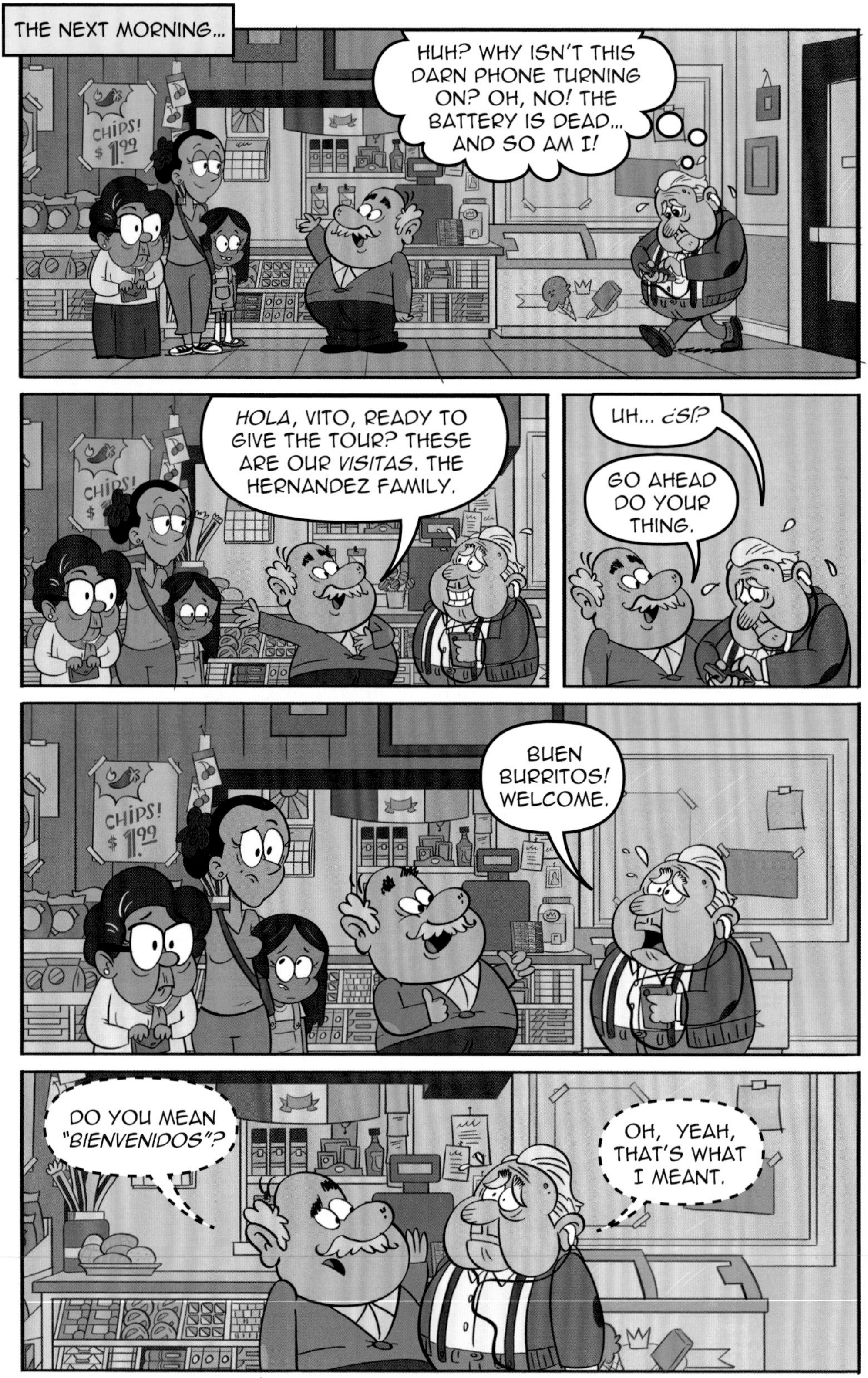
THE NEXT MORNING...
CHIPS! $1.99
HUH? WHY ISN'T THIS DARN PHONE TURNING ON? OH, NO! THE BATTERY IS DEAD... AND SO AM I!
HOLA, VITO, READY TO GIVE THE TOUR? THESE ARE OUR VISITAS. THE HERNANDEZ FAMILY.
UH... ¿SÍ?
GO AHEAD DO YOUR THING.
BUEN BURRITOS! WELCOME.
DO YOU MEAN "BIENVENIDOS"?
OH, YEAH, THAT'S WHAT I MEANT.

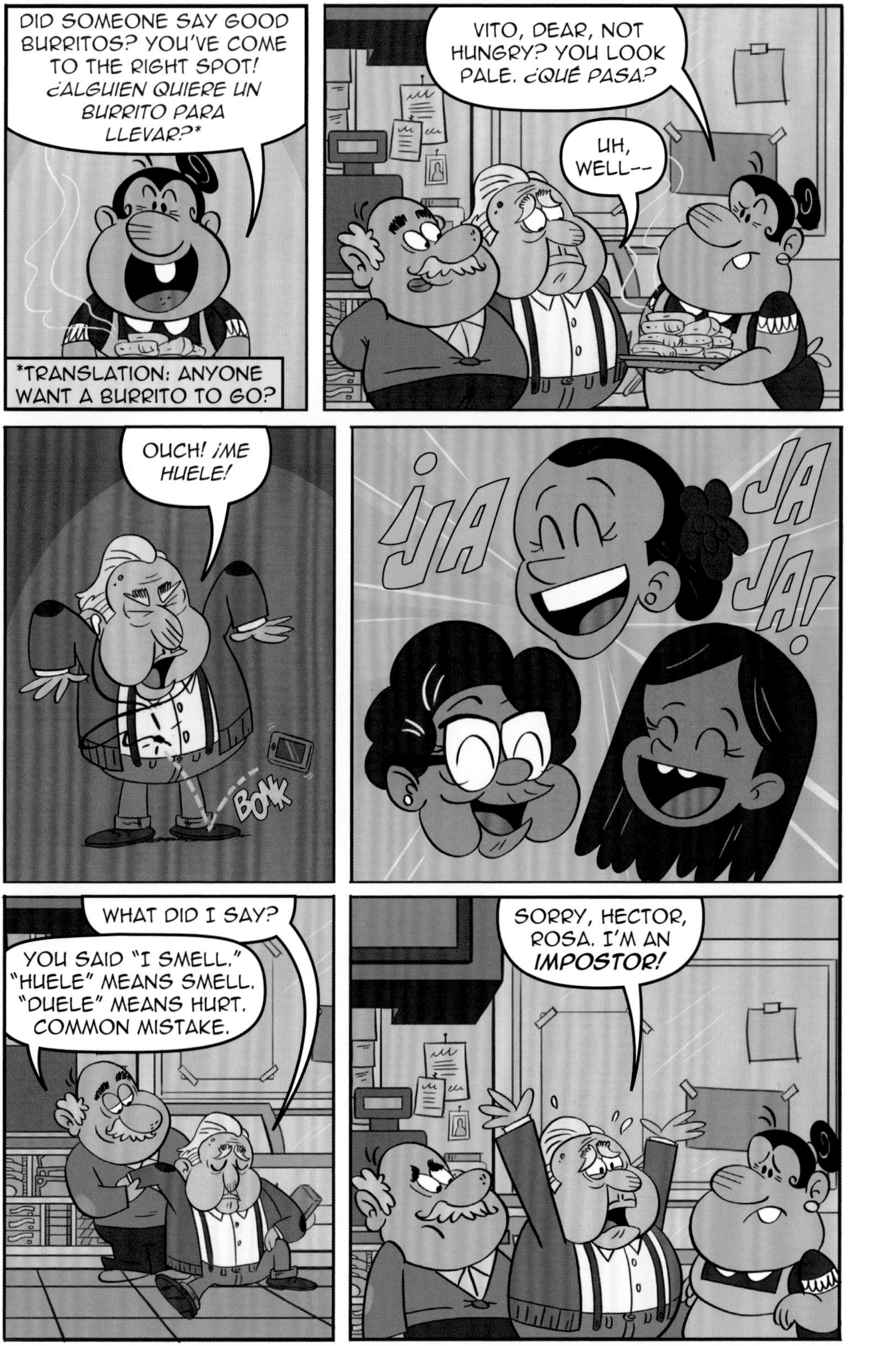
DID SOMEONE SAY GOOD BURRITOS? YOU'VE COME TO THE RIGHT SPOT! ¿ALGUIEN QUIERE UN BURRITO PARA LLEVAR?*
*TRANSLATION: ANYONE WANT A BURRITO TO GO?
VITO, DEAR, NOT HUNGRY? YOU LOOK PALE. ¿QUÉ PASA?
UH, WELL--
OUCH! ¡ME HUELE!
BONK
¡JA
JA
JA!
WHAT DID I SAY?
YOU SAID "I SMELL." "HUELE" MEANS SMELL. "DUELE" MEANS HURT. COMMON MISTAKE.
SORRY, HECTOR, ROSA. I'M AN *IMPOSTOR!*

ONE WEEK LATER...

HI, VITO. IT IS GOOD TO SEE YOU AGAIN, WE HAVEN'T SEEN YOU AROUND.

I'M SORRY ABOUT THE OTHER DAY. I JUST GOT CARRIED AWAY.

I THOUGHT I FOUND A SHORT CUT, BUT I SHOULD LEARN BY LISTENING, NOT USING A DOOHICKEY.

I GUESS I'LL NEVER LEARN SPANISH...

YOU'RE BEING TOO HARD ON YOURSELF. LEARNING A LANGUAGE TAKES TIME.

I'LL TAKE THIS *JAMÓN*, PLEASE.

VITO! THAT'S *SPANISH!* SEE? YOU'RE LEARNING!

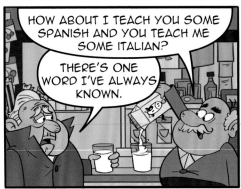

HOW ABOUT I TEACH YOU SOME SPANISH AND YOU TEACH ME SOME ITALIAN?

THERE'S ONE WORD I'VE ALWAYS KNOWN.

WHAT'S THAT?

AMIGO.

CLINK

THE END

"ZACH AND THE MEAN CHALK"

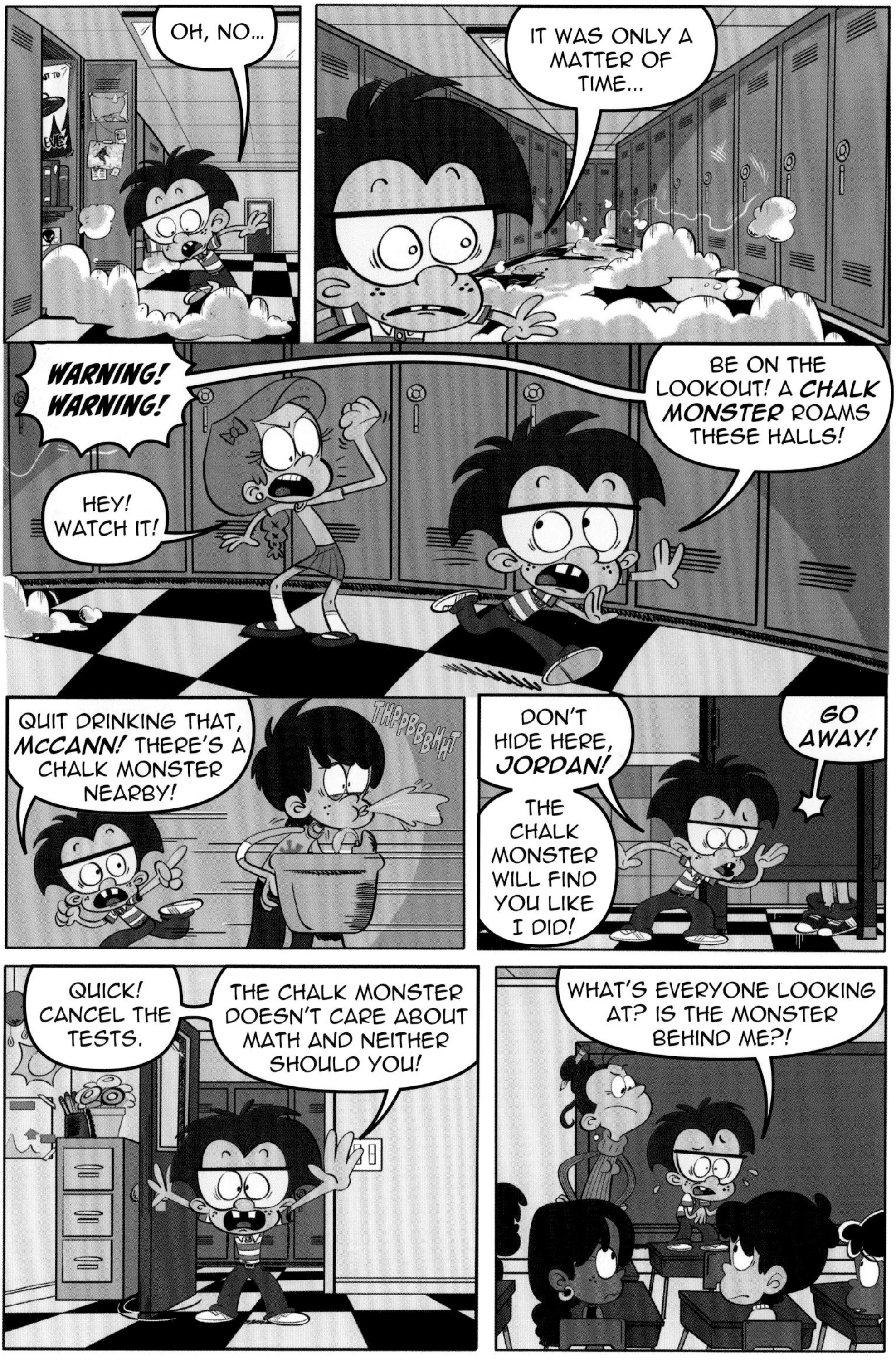

OH, NO...
IT WAS ONLY A MATTER OF TIME...
WARNING! WARNING!
BE ON THE LOOKOUT! A CHALK MONSTER ROAMS THESE HALLS!
HEY! WATCH IT!
QUIT DRINKING THAT, MCCANN! THERE'S A CHALK MONSTER NEARBY!
THPPBBBHHT
DON'T HIDE HERE, JORDAN!
THE CHALK MONSTER WILL FIND YOU LIKE I DID!
GO AWAY!
QUICK! CANCEL THE TESTS.
THE CHALK MONSTER DOESN'T CARE ABOUT MATH AND NEITHER SHOULD YOU!
WHAT'S EVERYONE LOOKING AT? IS THE MONSTER BEHIND ME?!

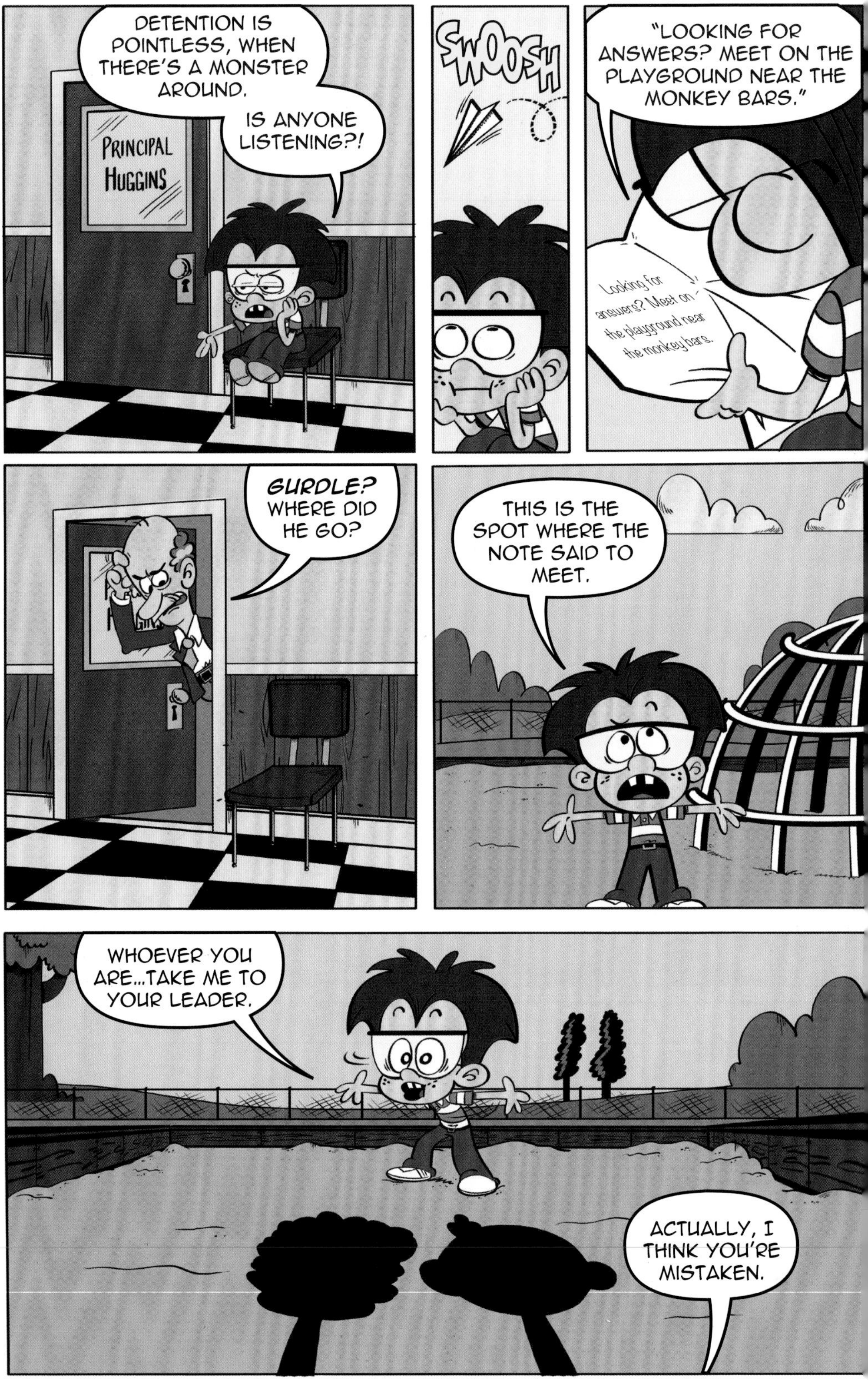

DETENTION IS POINTLESS, WHEN THERE'S A MONSTER AROUND.
IS ANYONE LISTENING?!
PRINCIPAL HUGGINS
SWOOSH
"LOOKING FOR ANSWERS? MEET ON THE PLAYGROUND NEAR THE MONKEY BARS."
Looking for answers? Meet on the playground near the monkey bars.
GURDLE? WHERE DID HE GO?
THIS IS THE SPOT WHERE THE NOTE SAID TO MEET.
WHOEVER YOU ARE...TAKE ME TO YOUR LEADER.
ACTUALLY, I THINK YOU'RE MISTAKEN.

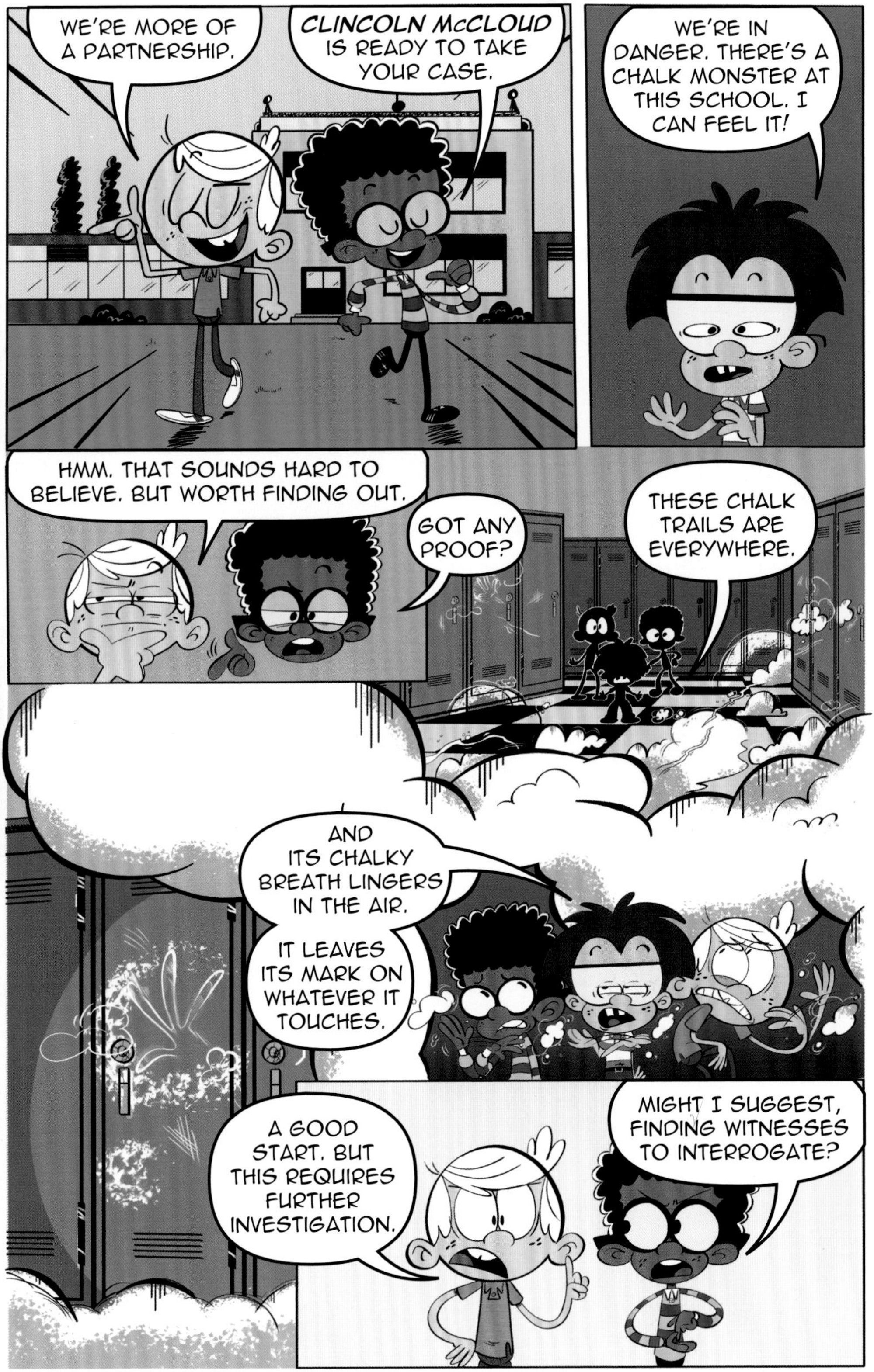

WE'RE MORE OF A PARTNERSHIP.
CLINCOLN McCLOUD IS READY TO TAKE YOUR CASE.
WE'RE IN DANGER. THERE'S A CHALK MONSTER AT THIS SCHOOL. I CAN FEEL IT!
HMM. THAT SOUNDS HARD TO BELIEVE. BUT WORTH FINDING OUT.
GOT ANY PROOF?
THESE CHALK TRAILS ARE EVERYWHERE.
AND ITS CHALKY BREATH LINGERS IN THE AIR.
IT LEAVES ITS MARK ON WHATEVER IT TOUCHES.
A GOOD START. BUT THIS REQUIRES FURTHER INVESTIGATION.
MIGHT I SUGGEST, FINDING WITNESSES TO INTERROGATE?

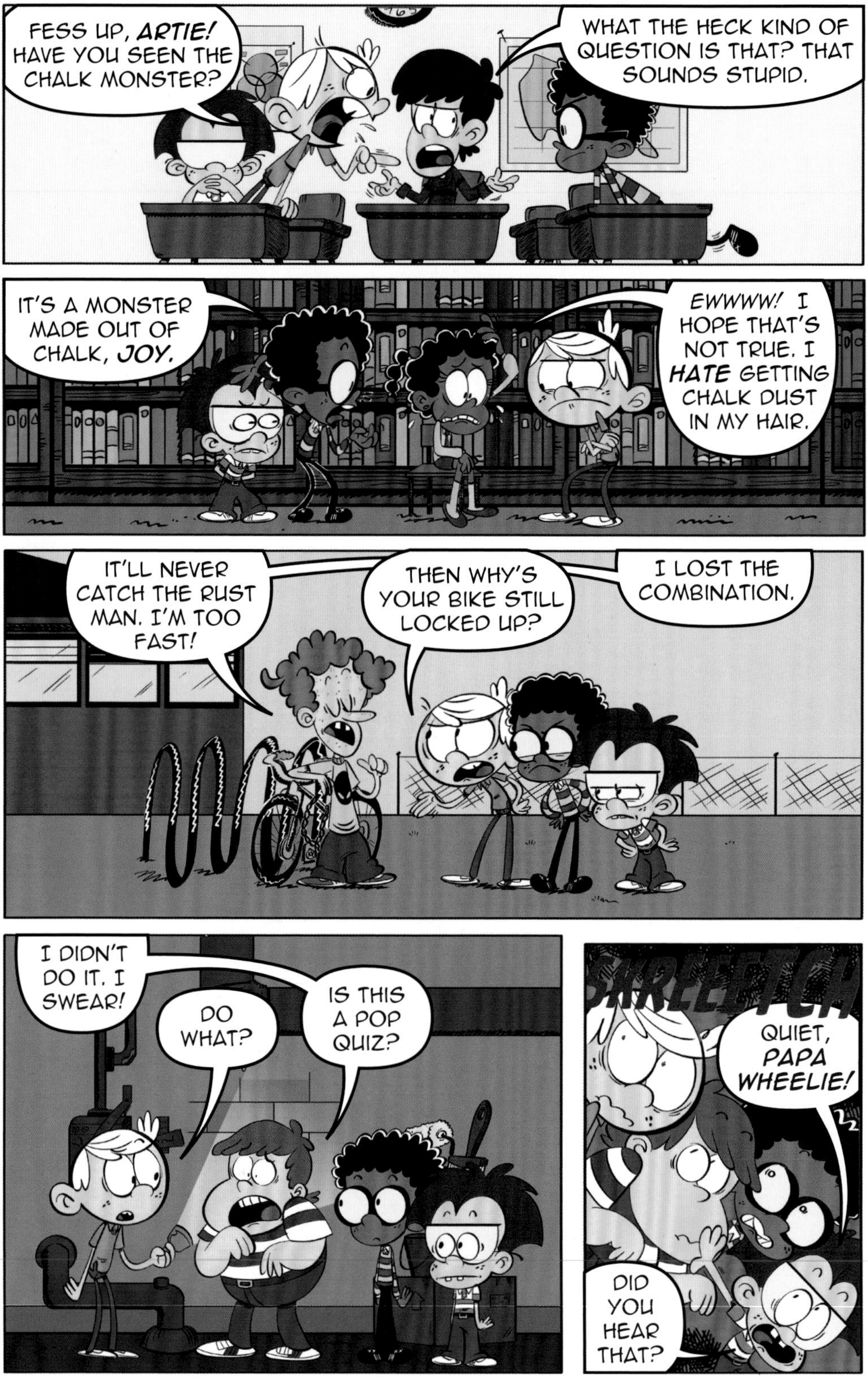
FESS UP, ARTIE! HAVE YOU SEEN THE CHALK MONSTER?
WHAT THE HECK KIND OF QUESTION IS THAT? THAT SOUNDS STUPID.
IT'S A MONSTER MADE OUT OF CHALK, JOY.
EWWWW! I HOPE THAT'S NOT TRUE. I HATE GETTING CHALK DUST IN MY HAIR.
IT'LL NEVER CATCH THE RUST MAN. I'M TOO FAST!
THEN WHY'S YOUR BIKE STILL LOCKED UP?
I LOST THE COMBINATION.
I DIDN'T DO IT. I SWEAR!
DO WHAT?
IS THIS A POP QUIZ?
SKREEEEETCH
QUIET, PAPA WHEELIE!
DID YOU HEAR THAT?

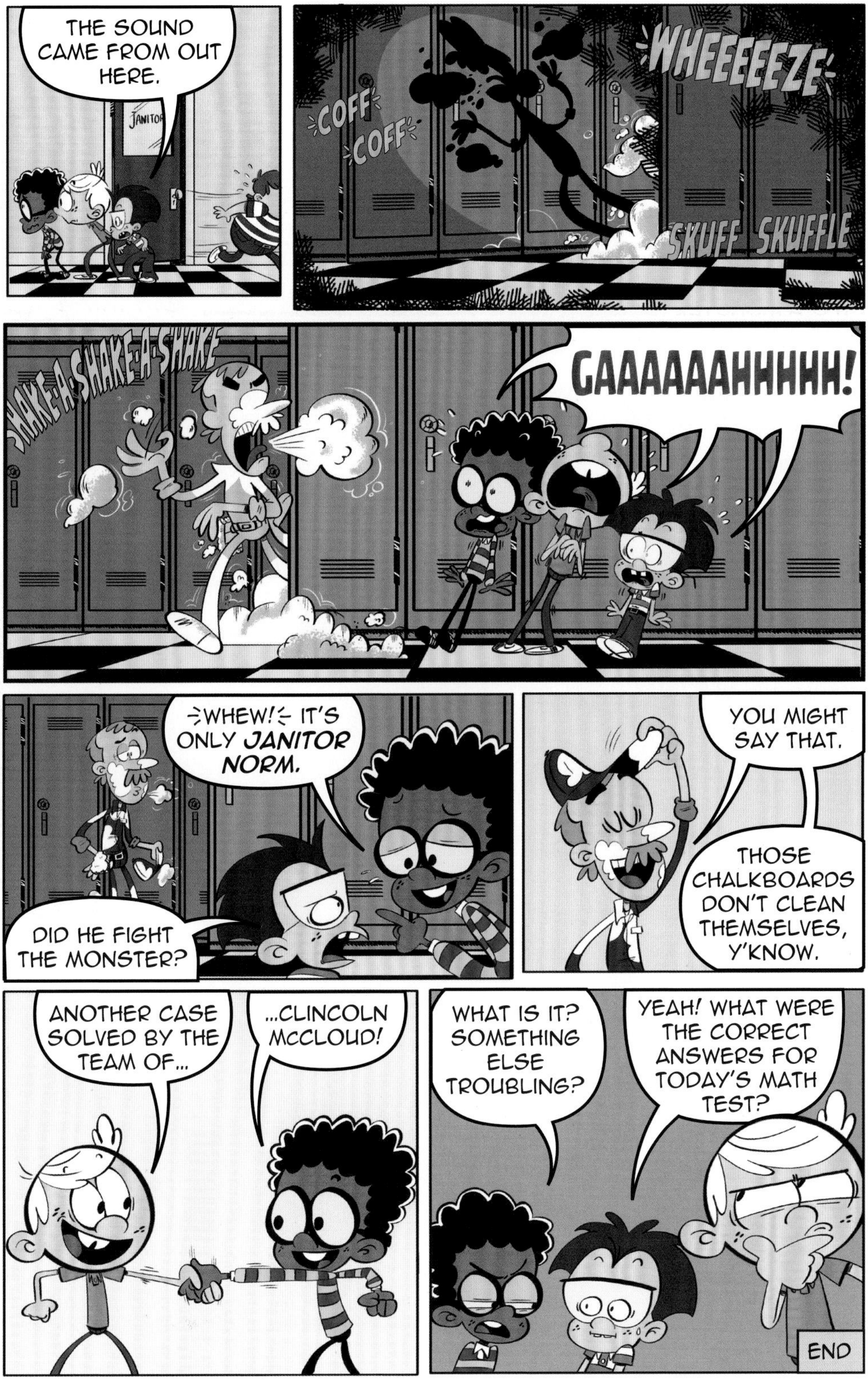
THE SOUND CAME FROM OUT HERE.
JANITOR
COFF
COFF
WHEEEEEEZE
SKUFF SKUFFLE
SHAKE-A-SHAKE-A-SHAKE
GAAAAAAHHHHH!
WHEW! IT'S ONLY JANITOR NORM.
DID HE FIGHT THE MONSTER?
YOU MIGHT SAY THAT.
THOSE CHALKBOARDS DON'T CLEAN THEMSELVES, Y'KNOW.
ANOTHER CASE SOLVED BY THE TEAM OF...
...CLINCOLN McCLOUD!
WHAT IS IT? SOMETHING ELSE TROUBLING?
YEAH! WHAT WERE THE CORRECT ANSWERS FOR TODAY'S MATH TEST?
END

"COMIC RELIEF"

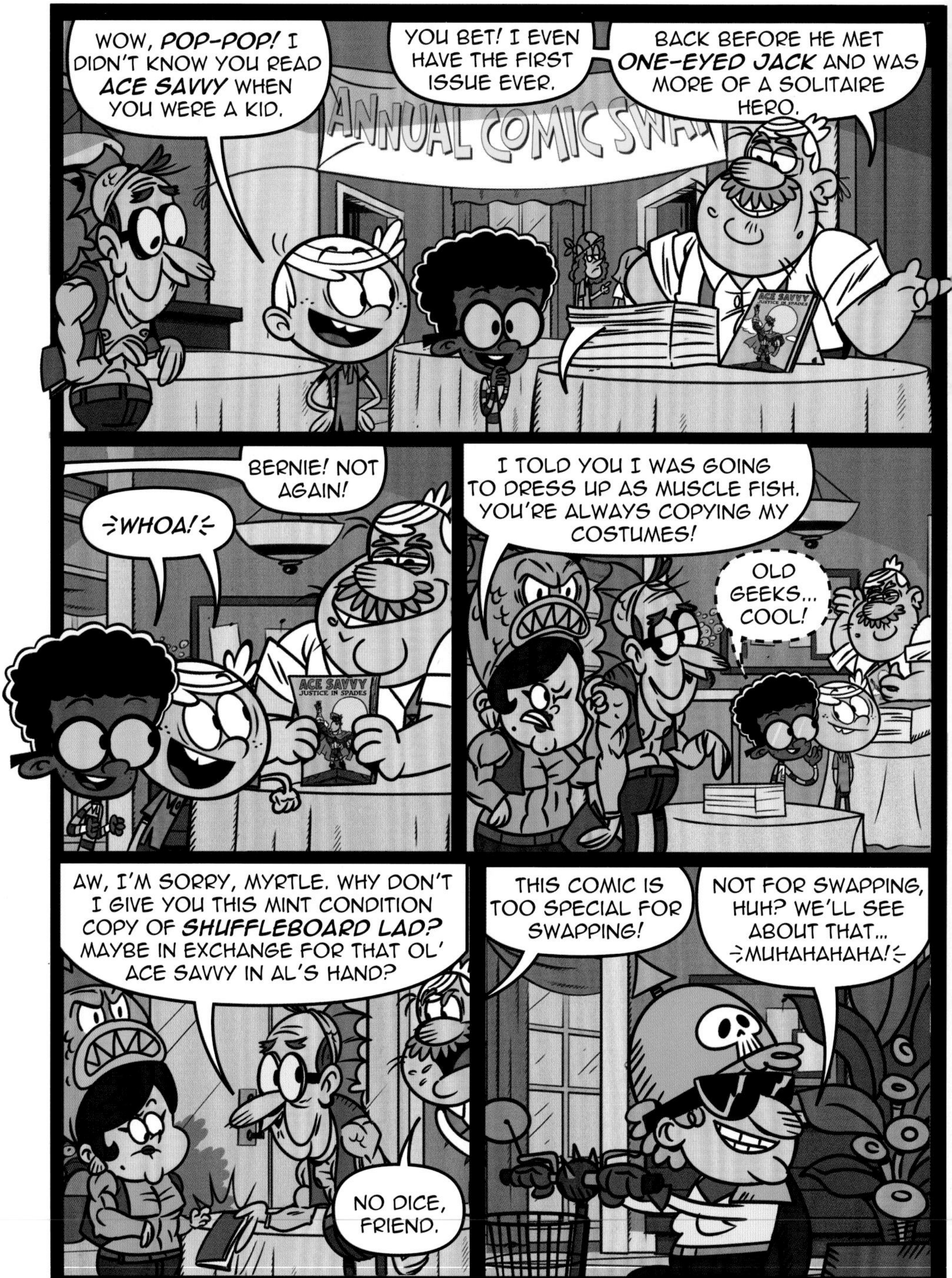
WOW, POP-POP! I DIDN'T KNOW YOU READ ACE SAVVY WHEN YOU WERE A KID.
YOU BET! I EVEN HAVE THE FIRST ISSUE EVER.
BACK BEFORE HE MET ONE-EYED JACK AND WAS MORE OF A SOLITAIRE HERO.
ANNUAL COMIC SWA
ACE SAVVY JUSTICE IN SPADES
BERNIE! NOT AGAIN!
WHOA!
I TOLD YOU I WAS GOING TO DRESS UP AS MUSCLE FISH. YOU'RE ALWAYS COPYING MY COSTUMES!
OLD GEEKS... COOL!
AW, I'M SORRY, MYRTLE. WHY DON'T I GIVE YOU THIS MINT CONDITION COPY OF SHUFFLEBOARD LAD? MAYBE IN EXCHANGE FOR THAT OL' ACE SAVVY IN AL'S HAND?
NO DICE, FRIEND.
THIS COMIC IS TOO SPECIAL FOR SWAPPING!
NOT FOR SWAPPING, HUH? WE'LL SEE ABOUT THAT... MUHAHAHAHA!

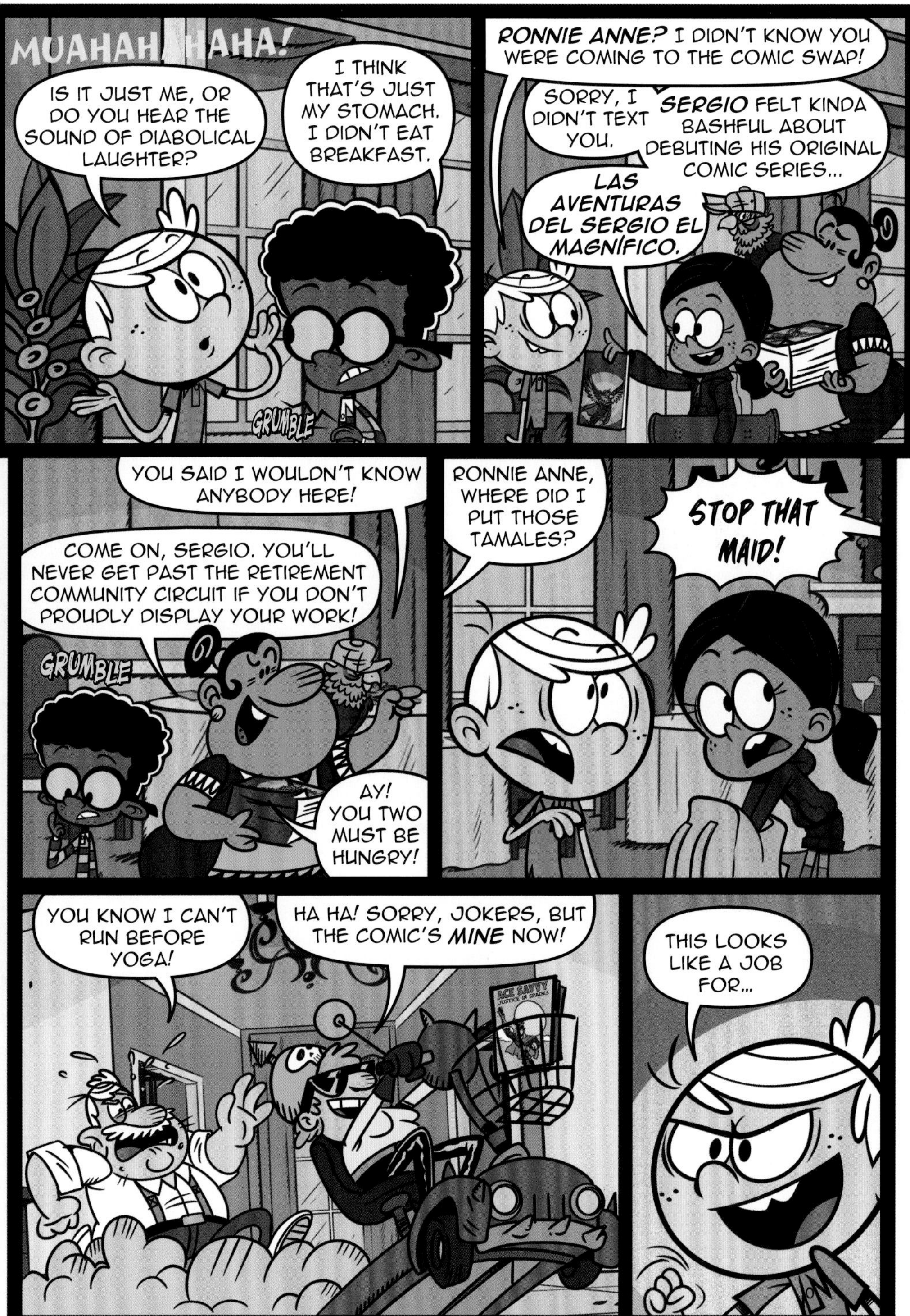
MUAHAHAHAHA!
IS IT JUST ME, OR DO YOU HEAR THE SOUND OF DIABOLICAL LAUGHTER?
I THINK THAT'S JUST MY STOMACH. I DIDN'T EAT BREAKFAST.
GRUMBLE
RONNIE ANNE? I DIDN'T KNOW YOU WERE COMING TO THE COMIC SWAP!
SORRY, I DIDN'T TEXT YOU.
SERGIO FELT KINDA BASHFUL ABOUT DEBUTING HIS ORIGINAL COMIC SERIES...
LAS AVENTURAS DEL SERGIO EL MAGNÍFICO.
YOU SAID I WOULDN'T KNOW ANYBODY HERE!
COME ON, SERGIO. YOU'LL NEVER GET PAST THE RETIREMENT COMMUNITY CIRCUIT IF YOU DON'T PROUDLY DISPLAY YOUR WORK!
GRUMBLE
AY! YOU TWO MUST BE HUNGRY!
RONNIE ANNE, WHERE DID I PUT THOSE TAMALES?
STOP THAT MAID!
YOU KNOW I CAN'T RUN BEFORE YOGA!
HA HA! SORRY, JOKERS, BUT THE COMIC'S MINE NOW!
ACE SAVVY
JUSTICE IN SPADES
THIS LOOKS LIKE A JOB FOR...

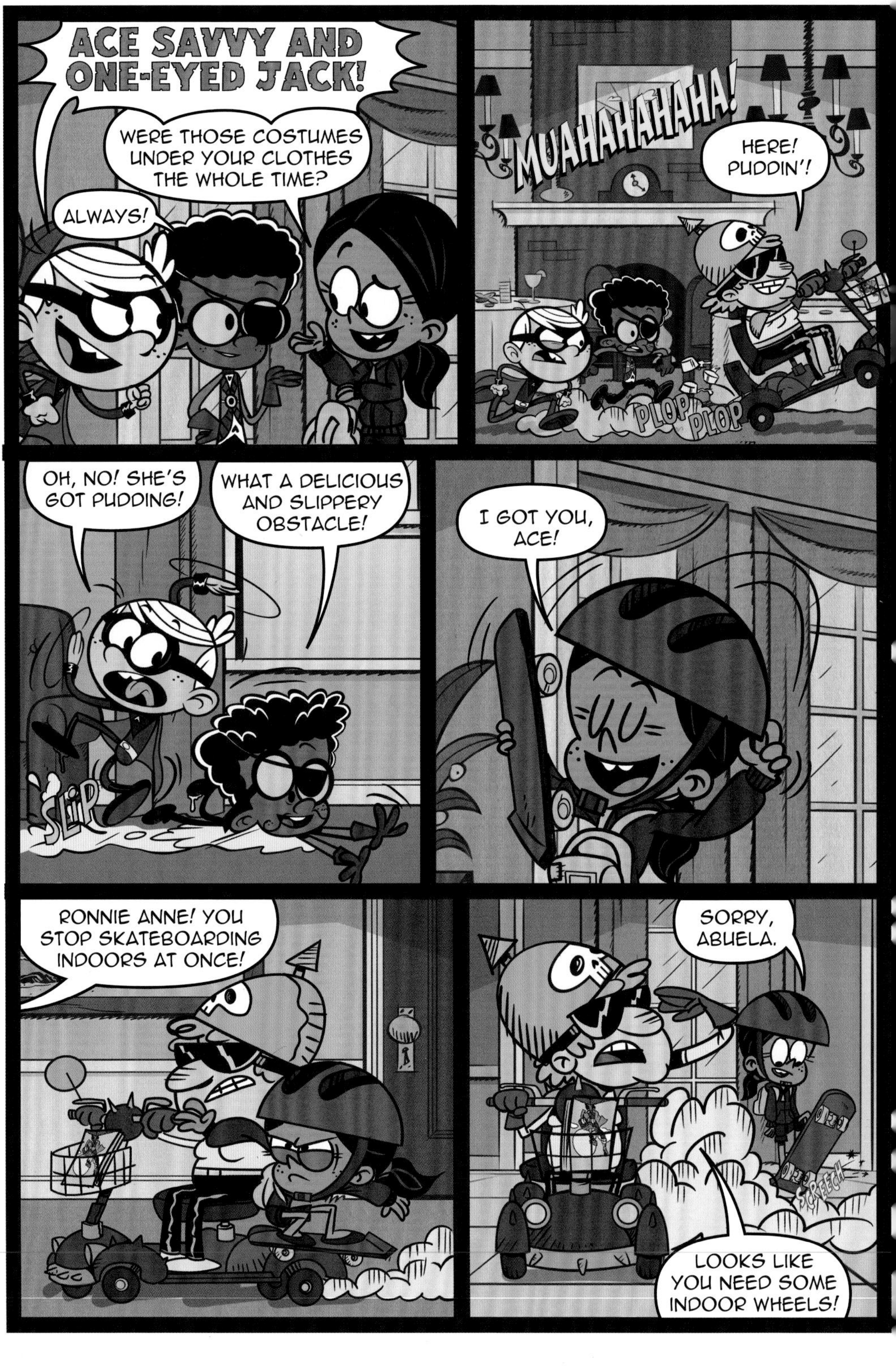
ACE SAVVY AND ONE-EYED JACK!
WERE THOSE COSTUMES UNDER YOUR CLOTHES THE WHOLE TIME?
ALWAYS!
MUAHAHAHAHA!
HERE! PUDDIN'!
PLOP
PLOP
OH, NO! SHE'S GOT PUDDING!
WHAT A DELICIOUS AND SLIPPERY OBSTACLE!
SLIP
I GOT YOU, ACE!
RONNIE ANNE! YOU STOP SKATEBOARDING INDOORS AT ONCE!
SORRY, ABUELA.
SCREECH
LOOKS LIKE YOU NEED SOME INDOOR WHEELS!

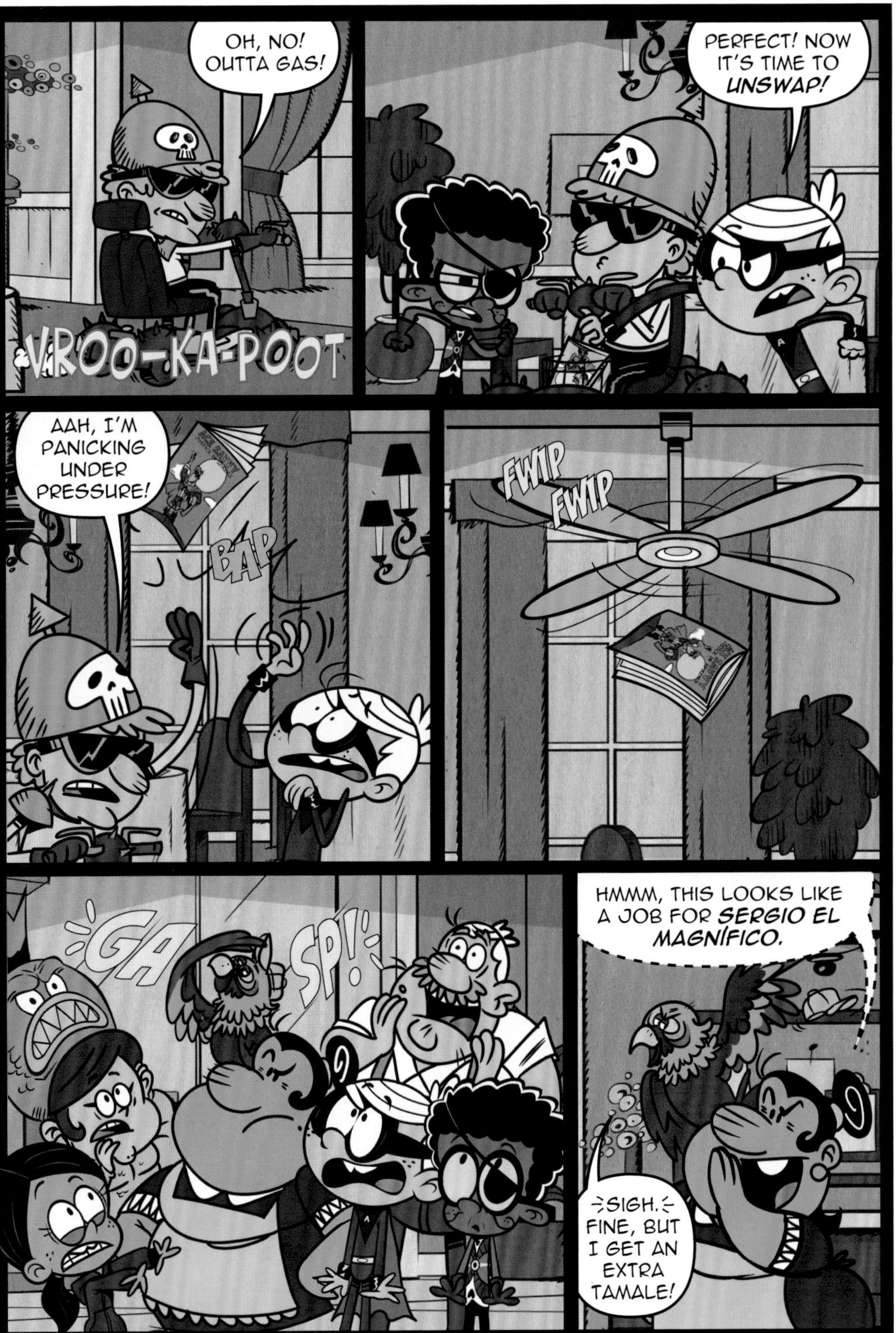
OH, NO!
OUTTA GAS!
VROO-KA-POOT
PERFECT! NOW IT'S TIME TO UNSWAP!
AAH, I'M PANICKING UNDER PRESSURE!
BAP
FWIP
FWIP
GASP!
HMMM, THIS LOOKS LIKE A JOB FOR SERGIO EL MAGNÍFICO.
SIGH. FINE, BUT I GET AN EXTRA TAMALE!

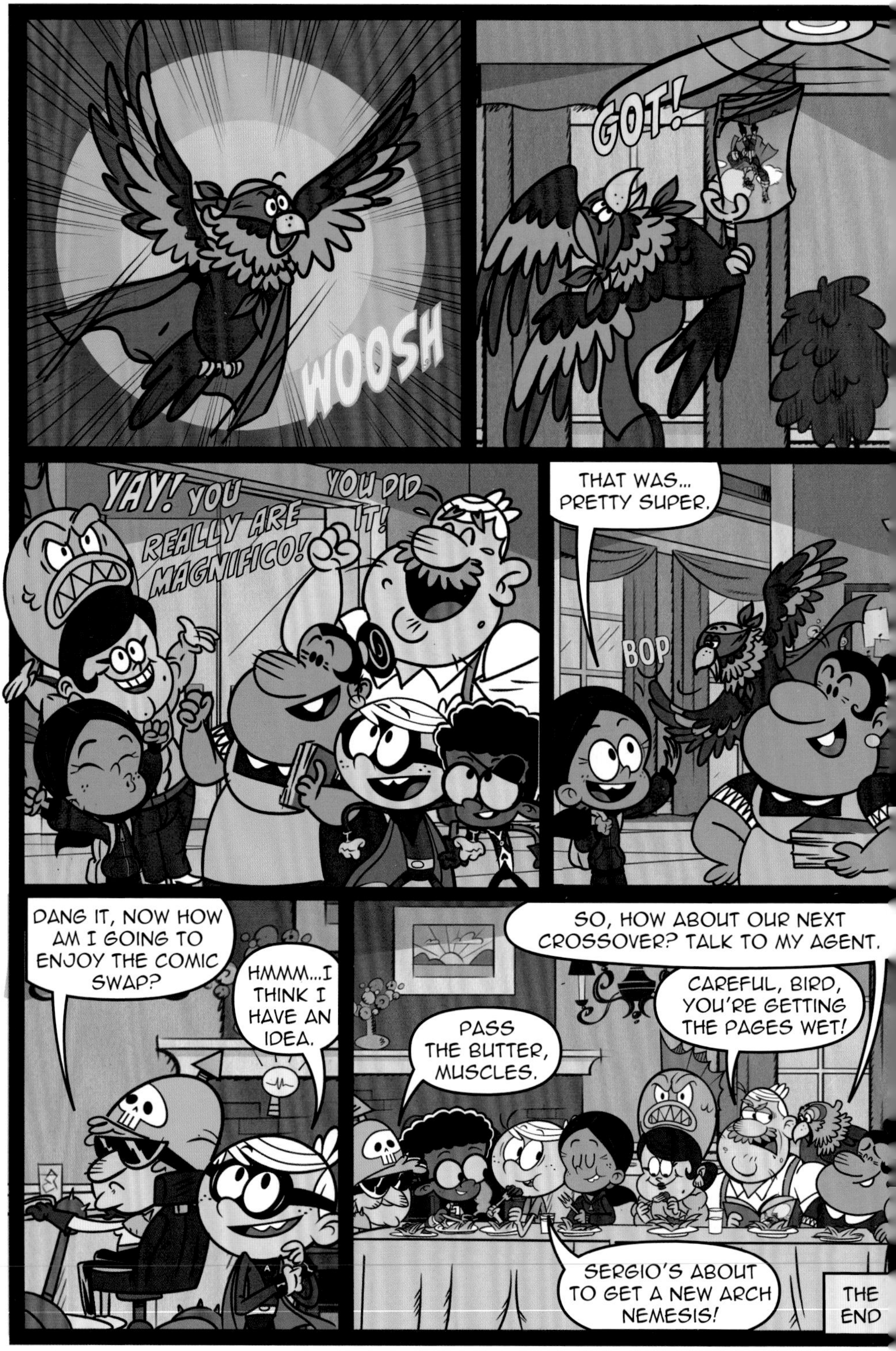
WOOSH
GOT!
YAY! YOU REALLY ARE MAGNIFICO!
YOU DID IT!
THAT WAS... PRETTY SUPER.
BOP
DANG IT, NOW HOW AM I GOING TO ENJOY THE COMIC SWAP?
HMMM...I THINK I HAVE AN IDEA.
SO, HOW ABOUT OUR NEXT CROSSOVER? TALK TO MY AGENT.
CAREFUL, BIRD, YOU'RE GETTING THE PAGES WET!
PASS THE BUTTER, MUSCLES.
SERGIO'S ABOUT TO GET A NEW ARCH NEMESIS!
THE END

"LEVEL UP"

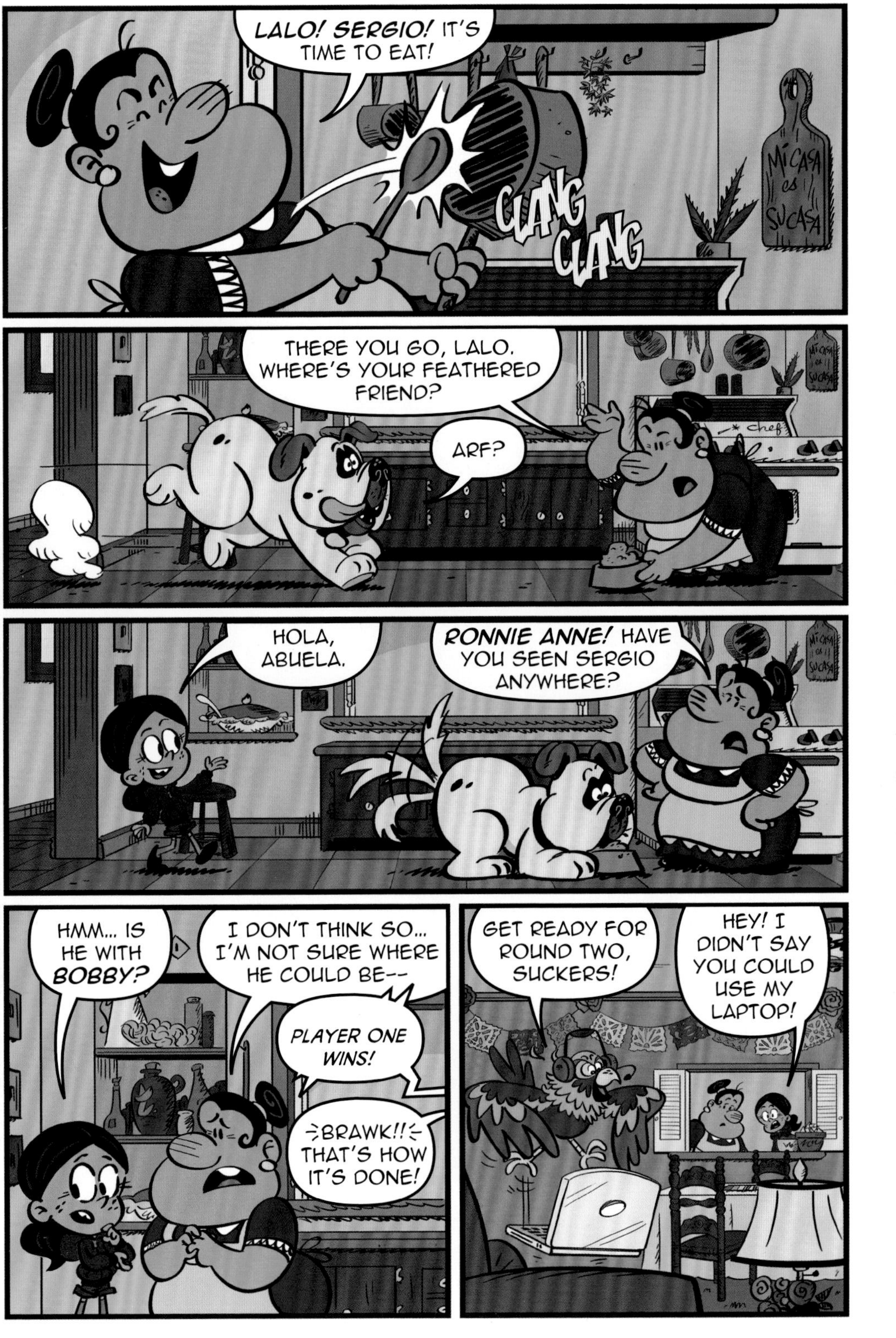
LALO! SERGIO! IT'S TIME TO EAT!
CLANG
CLANG
MÍ CASA es SU CASA
THERE YOU GO, LALO. WHERE'S YOUR FEATHERED FRIEND?
ARF?
HOLA, ABUELA.
RONNIE ANNE! HAVE YOU SEEN SERGIO ANYWHERE?
HMM... IS HE WITH BOBBY?
I DON'T THINK SO... I'M NOT SURE WHERE HE COULD BE--
PLAYER ONE WINS!
BRAWK!! THAT'S HOW IT'S DONE!
GET READY FOR ROUND TWO, SUCKERS!
HEY! I DIDN'T SAY YOU COULD USE MY LAPTOP!

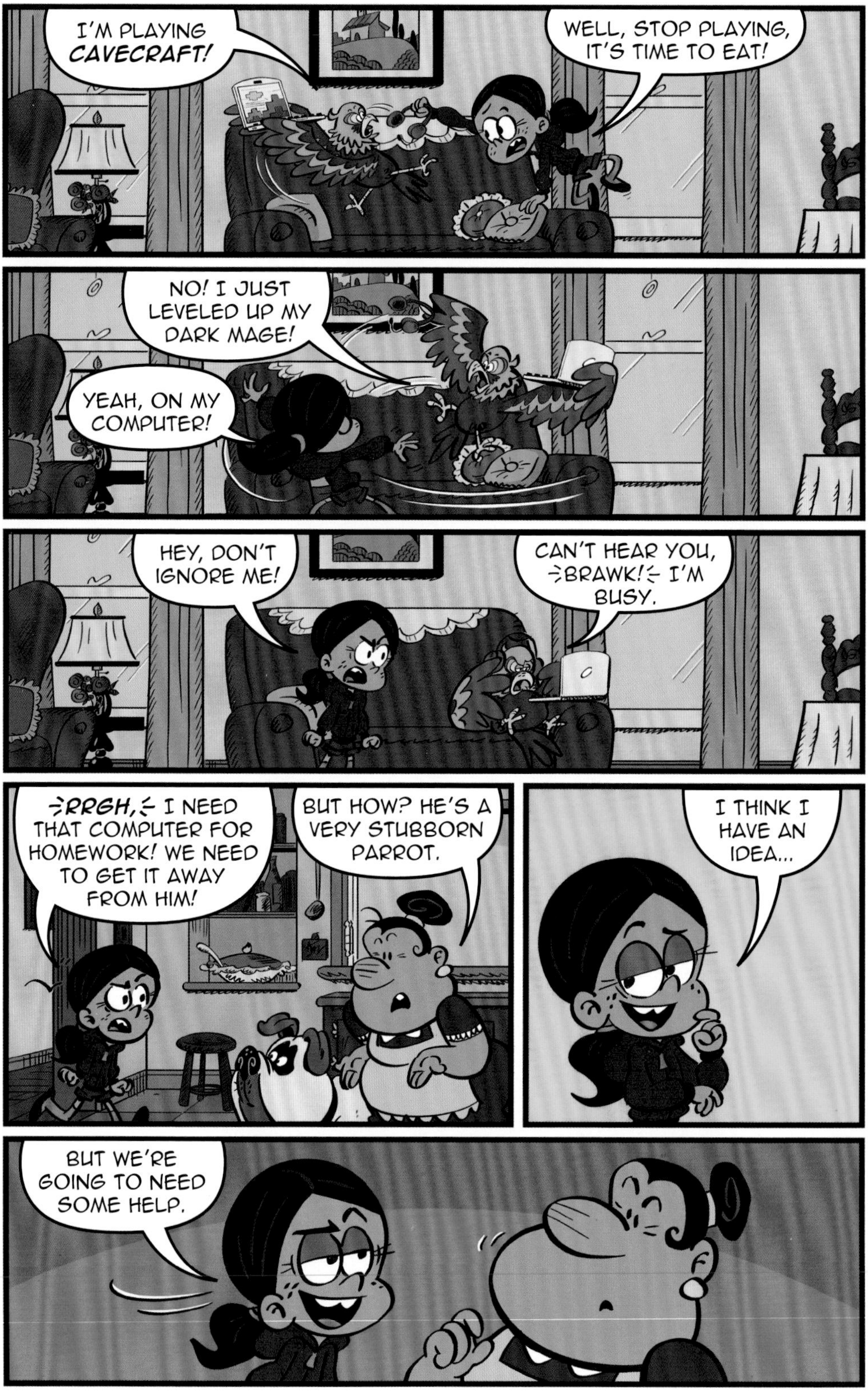
I'M PLAYING CAVECRAFT!
WELL, STOP PLAYING, IT'S TIME TO EAT!
NO! I JUST LEVELED UP MY DARK MAGE!
YEAH, ON MY COMPUTER!
HEY, DON'T IGNORE ME!
CAN'T HEAR YOU, BRAWK! I'M BUSY.
RRGH, I NEED THAT COMPUTER FOR HOMEWORK! WE NEED TO GET IT AWAY FROM HIM!
BUT HOW? HE'S A VERY STUBBORN PARROT.
I THINK I HAVE AN IDEA...
BUT WE'RE GOING TO NEED SOME HELP.

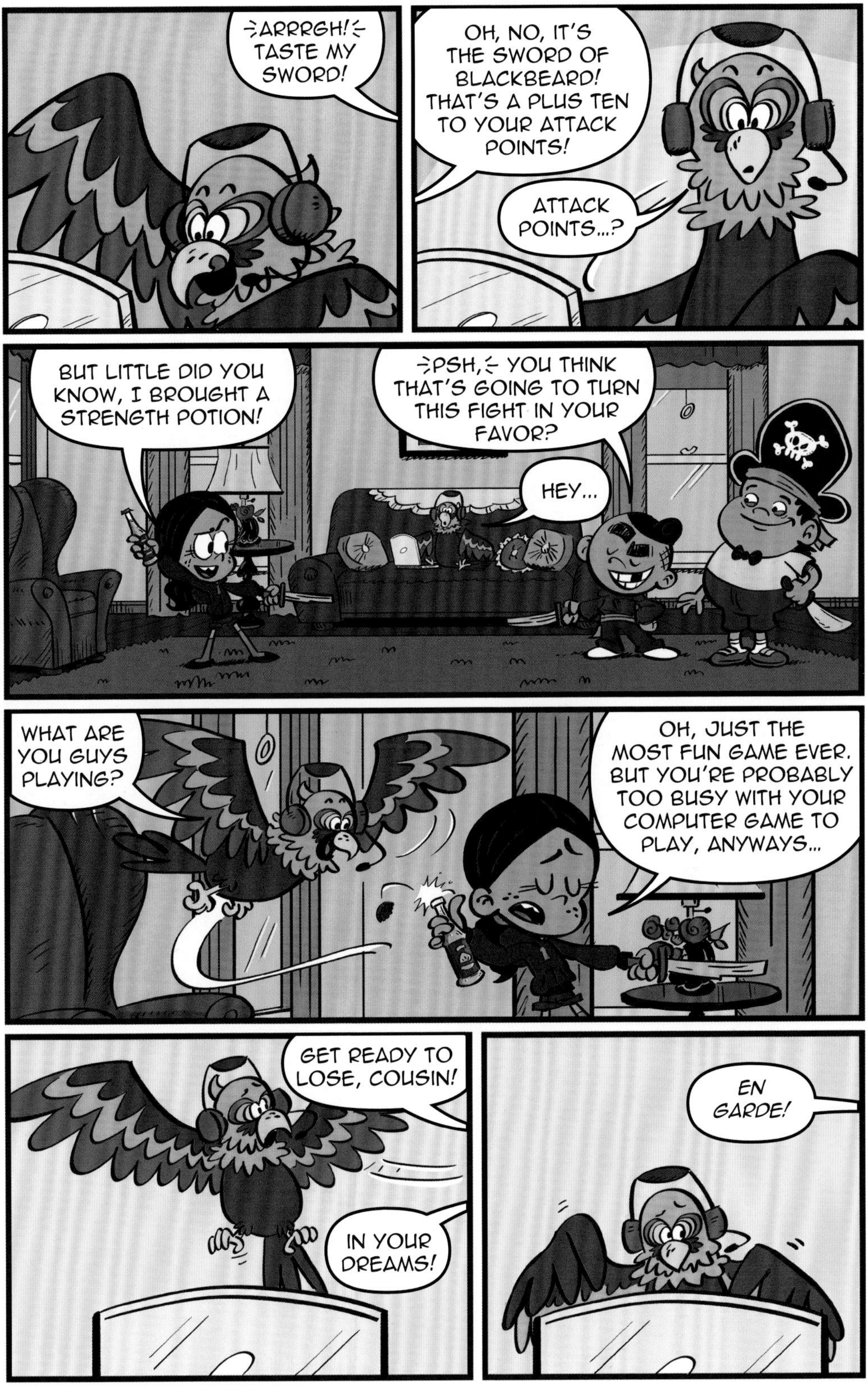
ARRRGH! TASTE MY SWORD!
OH, NO, IT'S THE SWORD OF BLACKBEARD! THAT'S A PLUS TEN TO YOUR ATTACK POINTS!
ATTACK POINTS...?
BUT LITTLE DID YOU KNOW, I BROUGHT A STRENGTH POTION!
PSH, YOU THINK THAT'S GOING TO TURN THIS FIGHT IN YOUR FAVOR?
HEY...
WHAT ARE YOU GUYS PLAYING?
OH, JUST THE MOST FUN GAME EVER. BUT YOU'RE PROBABLY TOO BUSY WITH YOUR COMPUTER GAME TO PLAY, ANYWAYS...
GET READY TO LOSE, COUSIN!
IN YOUR DREAMS!
EN GARDE!

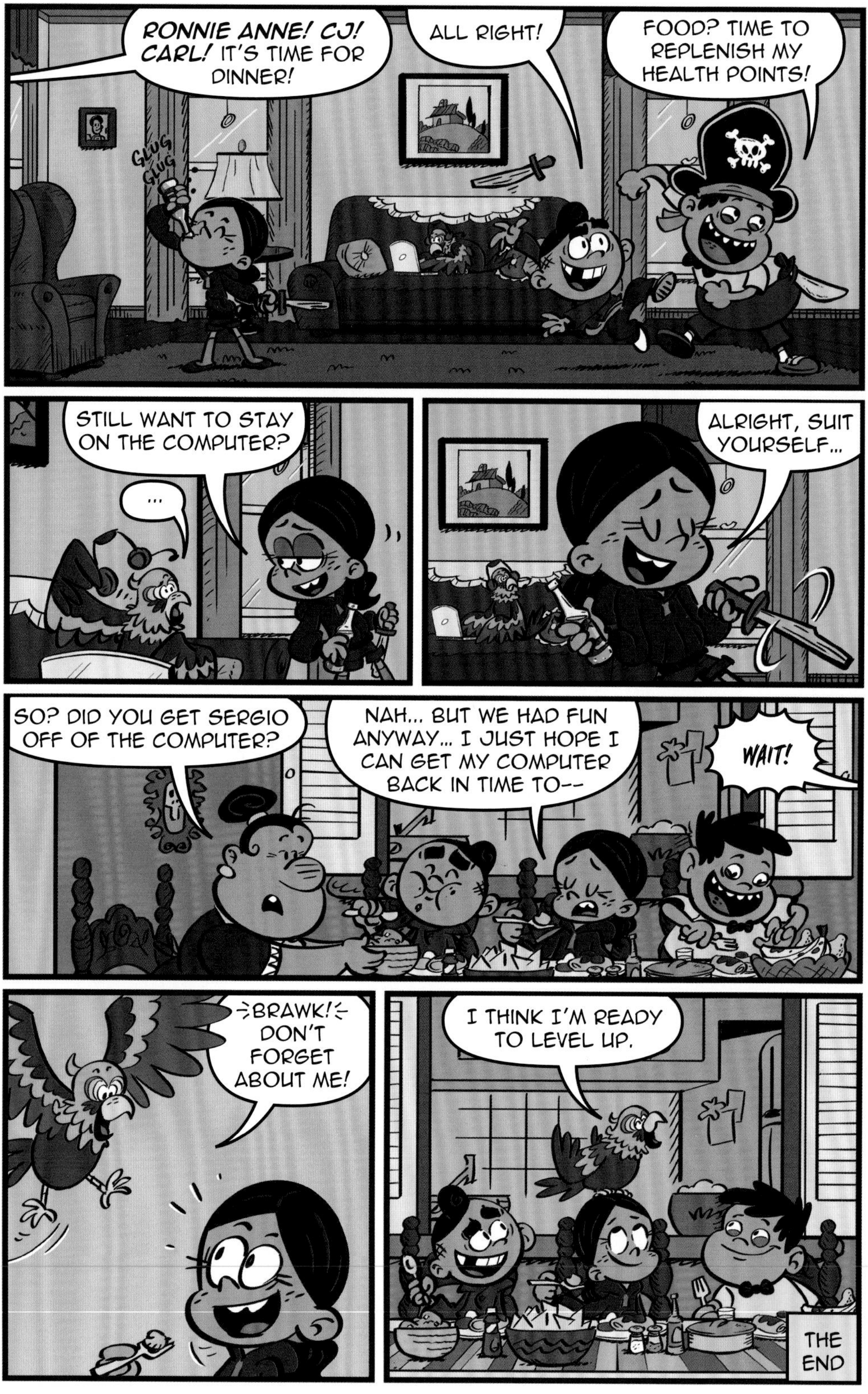
RONNIE ANNE! CJ! CARL! IT'S TIME FOR DINNER!
ALL RIGHT!
FOOD? TIME TO REPLENISH MY HEALTH POINTS!
GLUG GLUG
STILL WANT TO STAY ON THE COMPUTER?
...
ALRIGHT, SUIT YOURSELF...
SO? DID YOU GET SERGIO OFF OF THE COMPUTER?
NAH... BUT WE HAD FUN ANYWAY... I JUST HOPE I CAN GET MY COMPUTER BACK IN TIME TO--
WAIT!
BRAWK! DON'T FORGET ABOUT ME!
I THINK I'M READY TO LEVEL UP.
THE END

"MEAT YOUR MAKER"

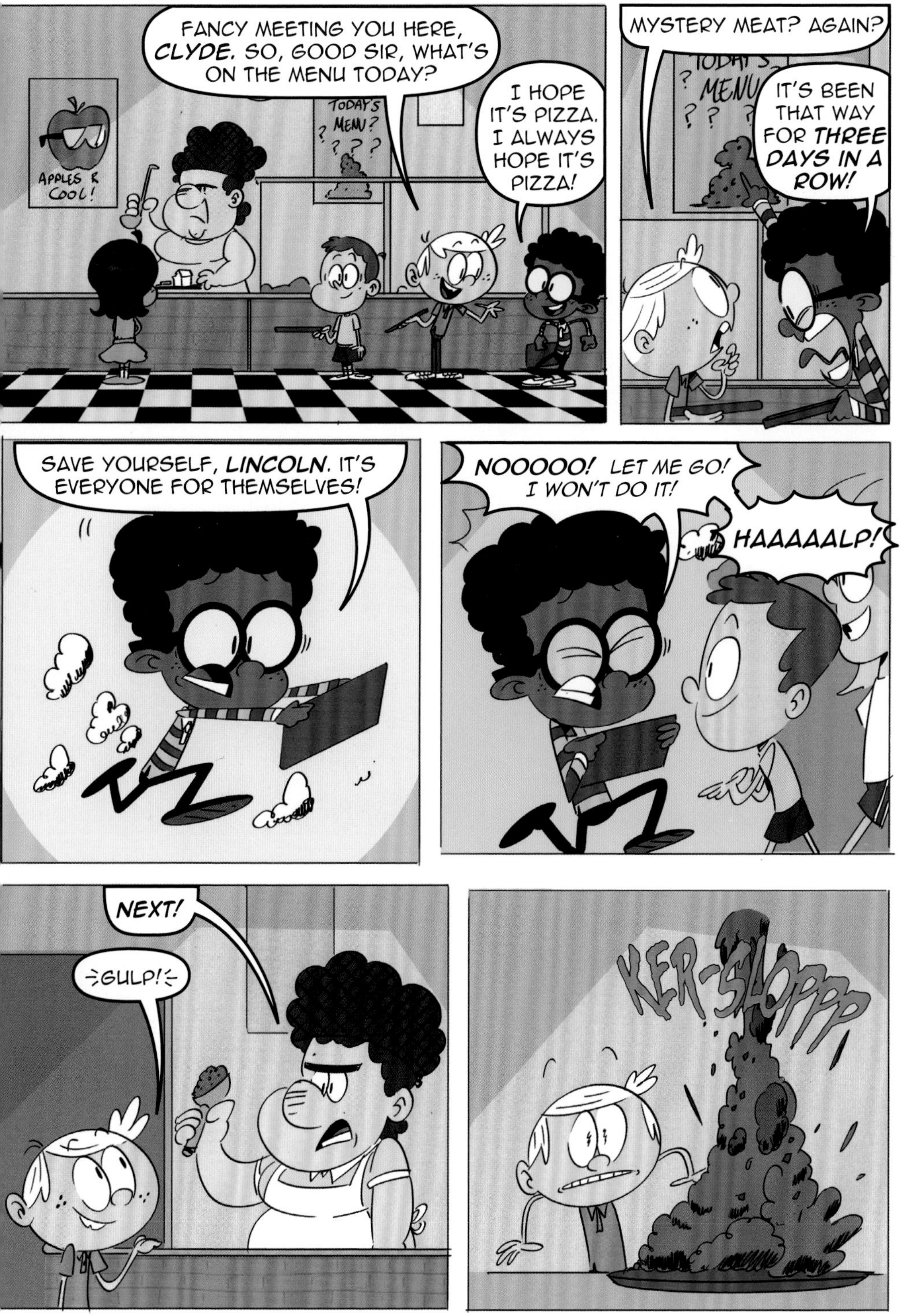

FANCY MEETING YOU HERE, CLYDE. SO, GOOD SIR, WHAT'S ON THE MENU TODAY?
APPLES R COOL!
TODAY'S MENU? ? ? ? ?
I HOPE IT'S PIZZA. I ALWAYS HOPE IT'S PIZZA!
MYSTERY MEAT? AGAIN?
IT'S BEEN THAT WAY FOR THREE DAYS IN A ROW!
SAVE YOURSELF, LINCOLN. IT'S EVERYONE FOR THEMSELVES!
NOOOOO! LET ME GO! I WON'T DO IT!
HAAAAALP!
NEXT!
GULP!
KER-SLOPPP

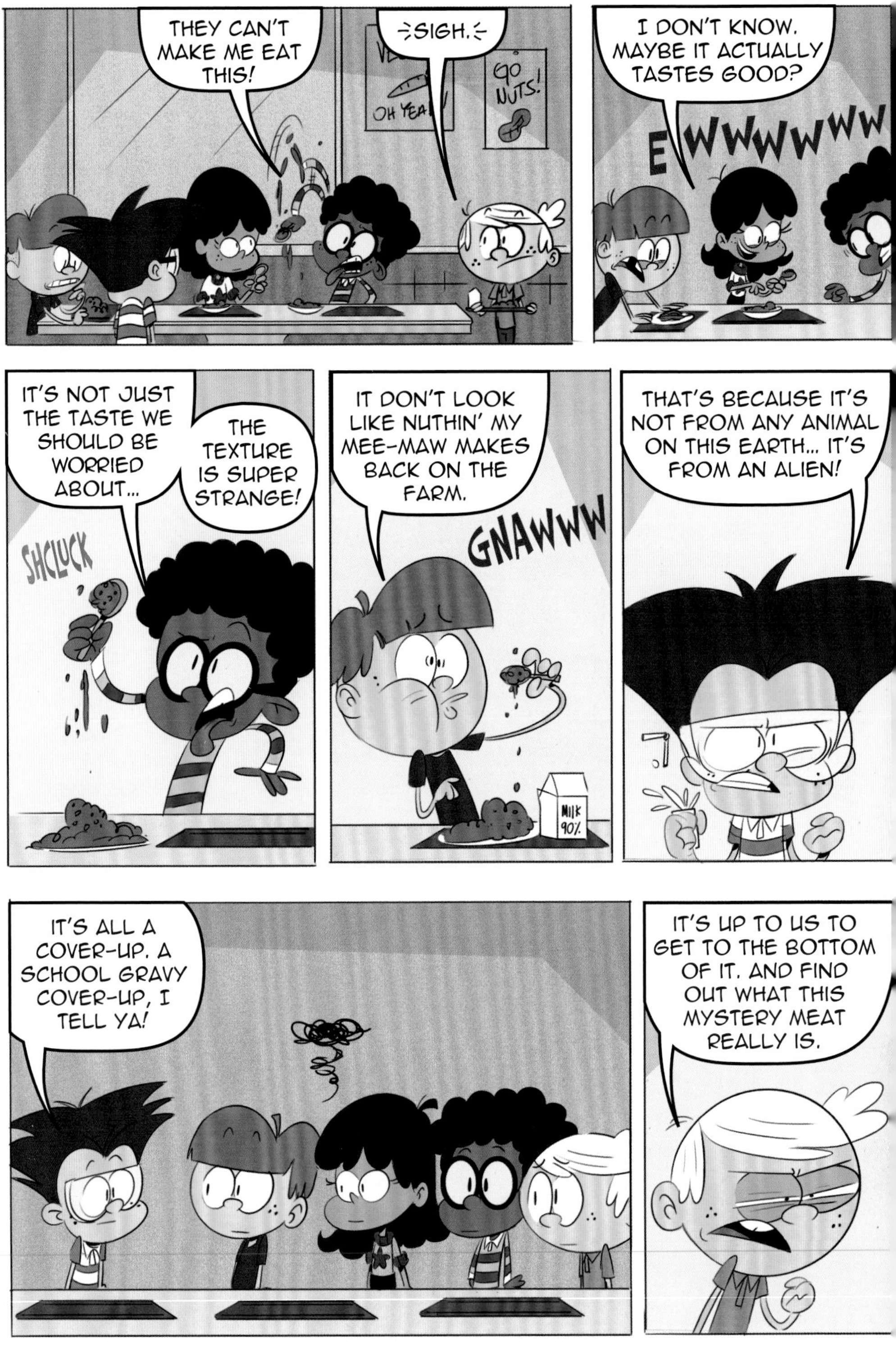
THEY CAN'T MAKE ME EAT THIS!
SIGH.
OH YEAH!
GO NUTS!
I DON'T KNOW. MAYBE IT ACTUALLY TASTES GOOD?
EWWWWWWW
IT'S NOT JUST THE TASTE WE SHOULD BE WORRIED ABOUT...
THE TEXTURE IS SUPER STRANGE!
SHCLUCK
IT DON'T LOOK LIKE NUTHIN' MY MEE-MAW MAKES BACK ON THE FARM.
GNAWWW
MILK 90%
THAT'S BECAUSE IT'S NOT FROM ANY ANIMAL ON THIS EARTH... IT'S FROM AN ALIEN!
IT'S ALL A COVER-UP. A SCHOOL GRAVY COVER-UP, I TELL YA!
IT'S UP TO US TO GET TO THE BOTTOM OF IT. AND FIND OUT WHAT THIS MYSTERY MEAT REALLY IS.

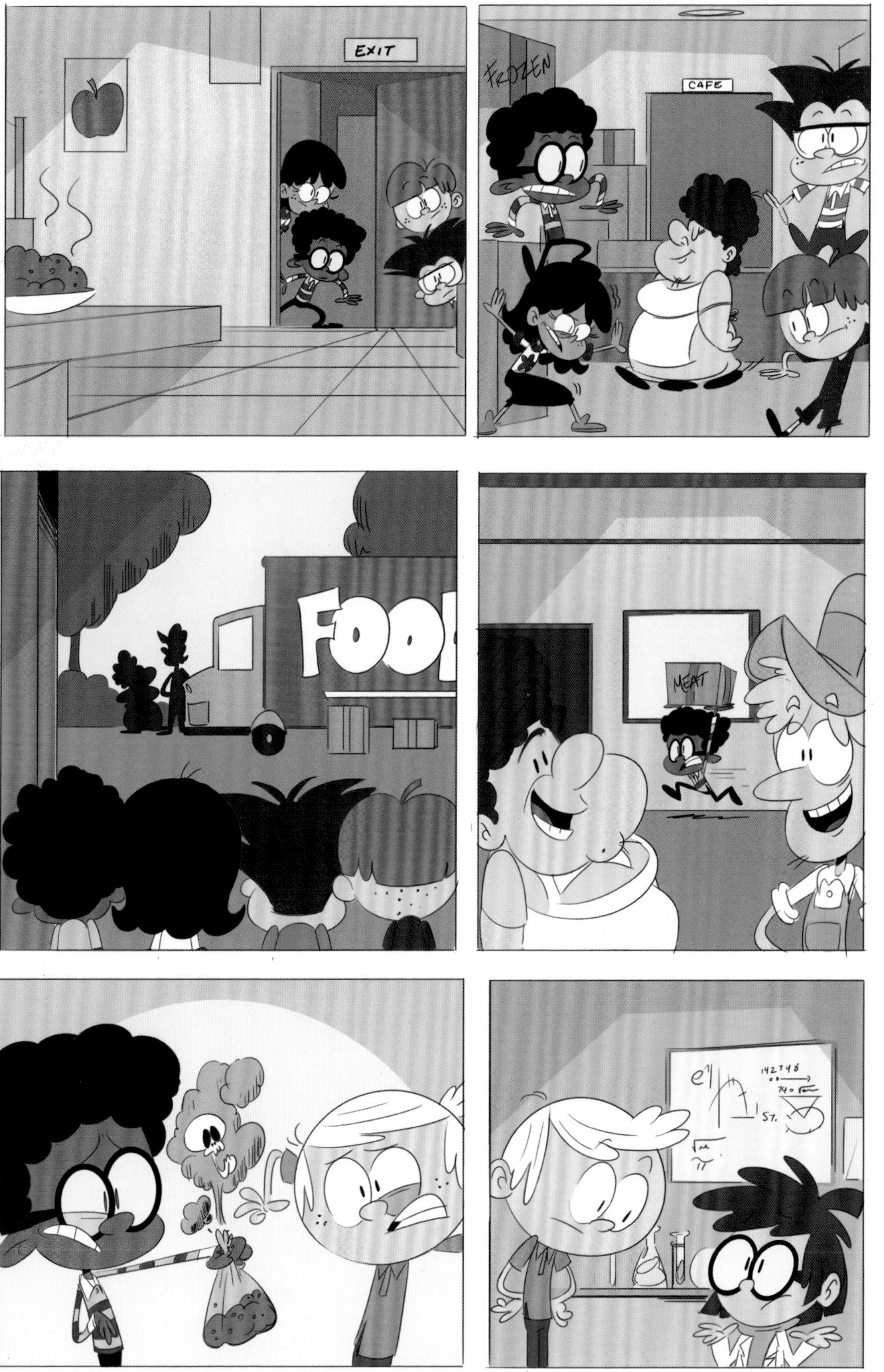
EXIT
FROZEN
CAFE
FOO
MEAT

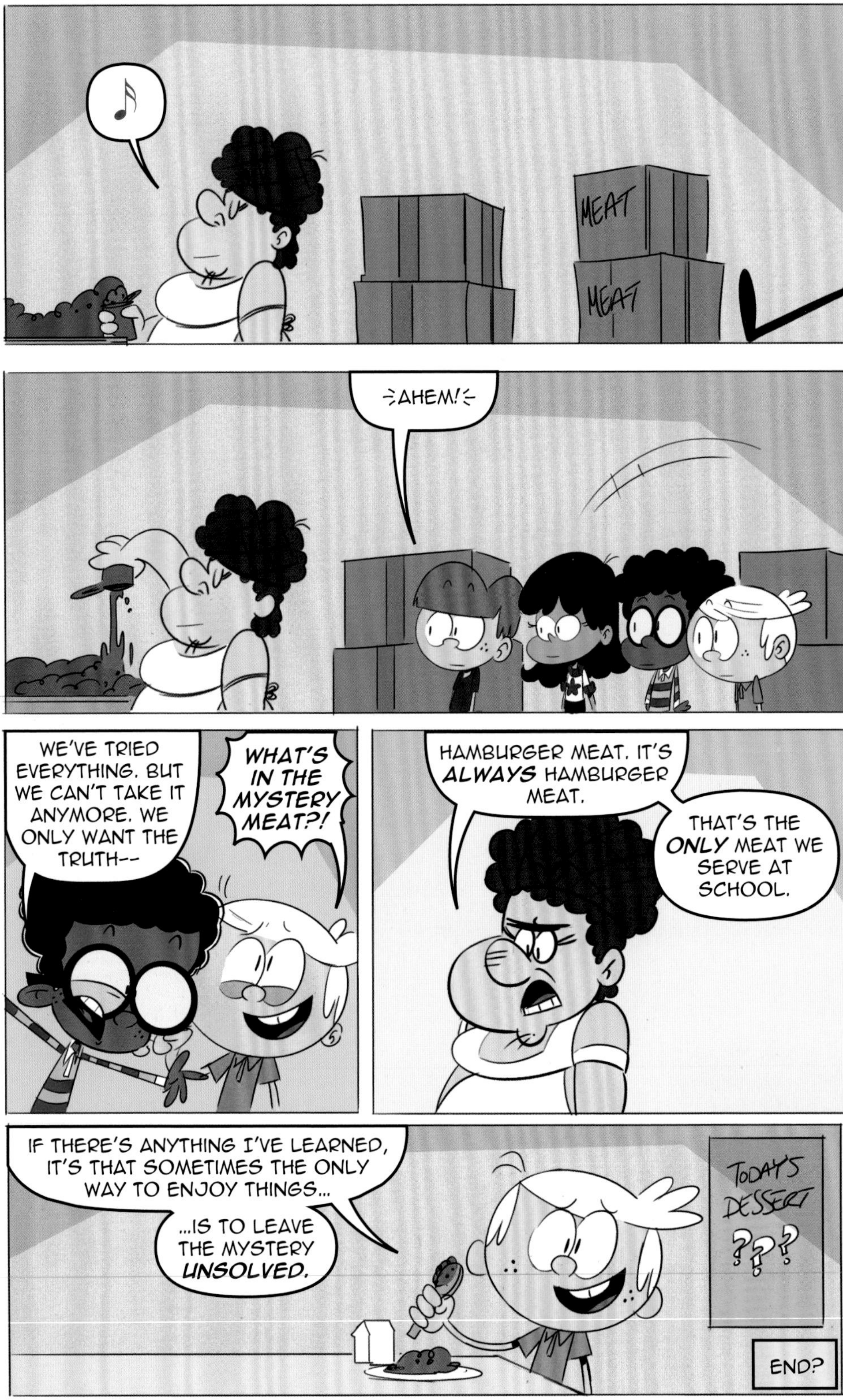
♪
AHEM!
WE'VE TRIED EVERYTHING. BUT WE CAN'T TAKE IT ANYMORE. WE ONLY WANT THE TRUTH--
WHAT'S IN THE MYSTERY MEAT?!
HAMBURGER MEAT. IT'S ALWAYS HAMBURGER MEAT.
THAT'S THE ONLY MEAT WE SERVE AT SCHOOL.
IF THERE'S ANYTHING I'VE LEARNED, IT'S THAT SOMETIMES THE ONLY WAY TO ENJOY THINGS...
...IS TO LEAVE THE MYSTERY UNSOLVED.
TODAY'S DESSERT ???
END?

"MODEL PETS"

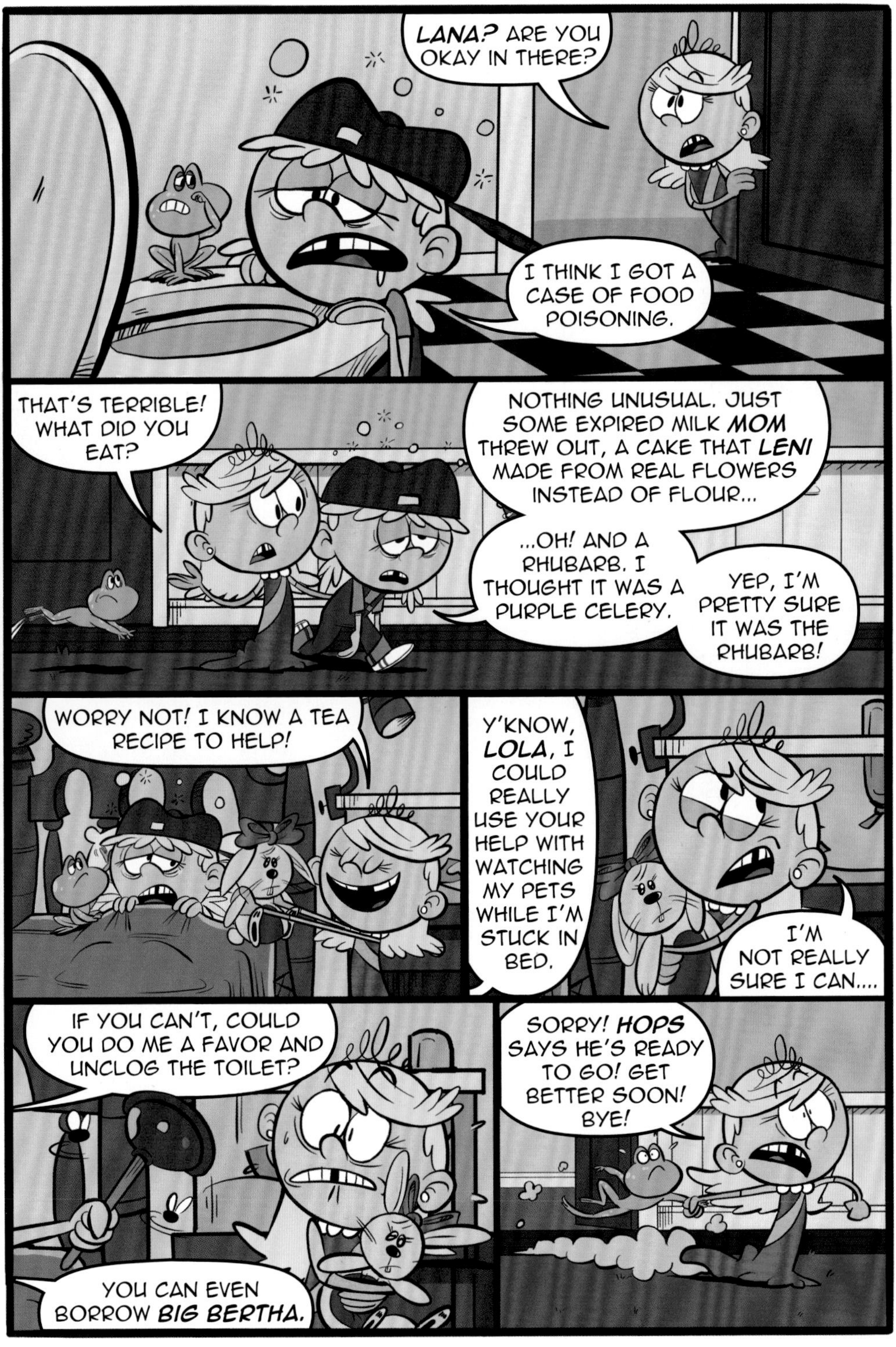
LANA? ARE YOU OKAY IN THERE?
I THINK I GOT A CASE OF FOOD POISONING.
THAT'S TERRIBLE! WHAT DID YOU EAT?
NOTHING UNUSUAL. JUST SOME EXPIRED MILK MOM THREW OUT, A CAKE THAT LENI MADE FROM REAL FLOWERS INSTEAD OF FLOUR...
...OH! AND A RHUBARB. I THOUGHT IT WAS A PURPLE CELERY.
YEP, I'M PRETTY SURE IT WAS THE RHUBARB!
WORRY NOT! I KNOW A TEA RECIPE TO HELP!
Y'KNOW, LOLA, I COULD REALLY USE YOUR HELP WITH WATCHING MY PETS WHILE I'M STUCK IN BED.
I'M NOT REALLY SURE I CAN....
IF YOU CAN'T, COULD YOU DO ME A FAVOR AND UNCLOG THE TOILET?
YOU CAN EVEN BORROW BIG BERTHA.
SORRY! HOPS SAYS HE'S READY TO GO! GET BETTER SOON! BYE!

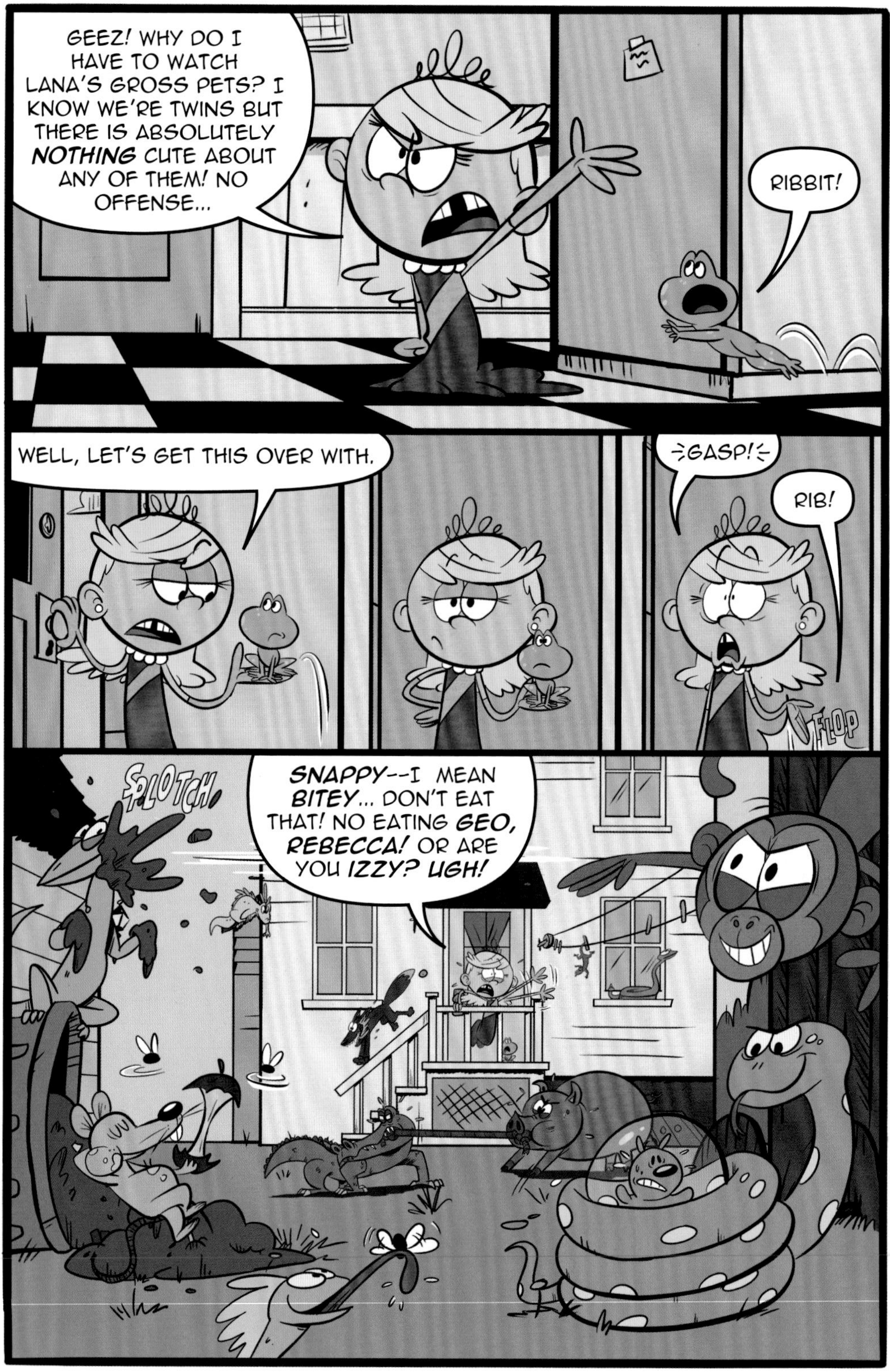
GEEZ! WHY DO I HAVE TO WATCH LANA'S GROSS PETS? I KNOW WE'RE TWINS BUT THERE IS ABSOLUTELY NOTHING CUTE ABOUT ANY OF THEM! NO OFFENSE...
RIBBIT!
WELL, LET'S GET THIS OVER WITH.
GASP!
RIB!
FLOP
SPLOTCH
SNAPPY--I MEAN BITEY... DON'T EAT THAT! NO EATING GEO, REBECCA! OR ARE YOU IZZY? UGH!

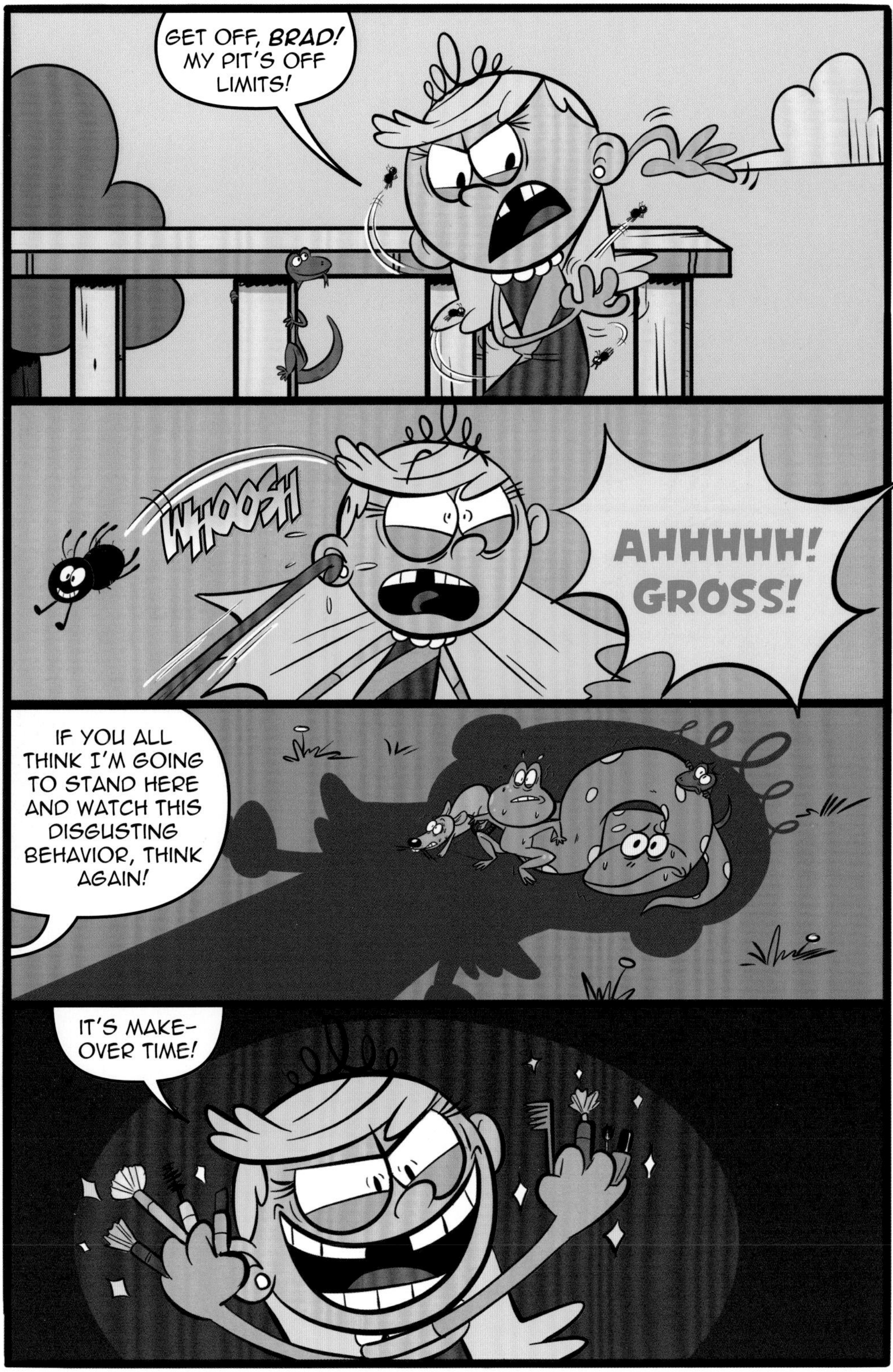
GET OFF, BRAD! MY PIT'S OFF LIMITS!
WHOOSH
AHHHHH! GROSS!
IF YOU ALL THINK I'M GOING TO STAND HERE AND WATCH THIS DISGUSTING BEHAVIOR, THINK AGAIN!
IT'S MAKE-OVER TIME!

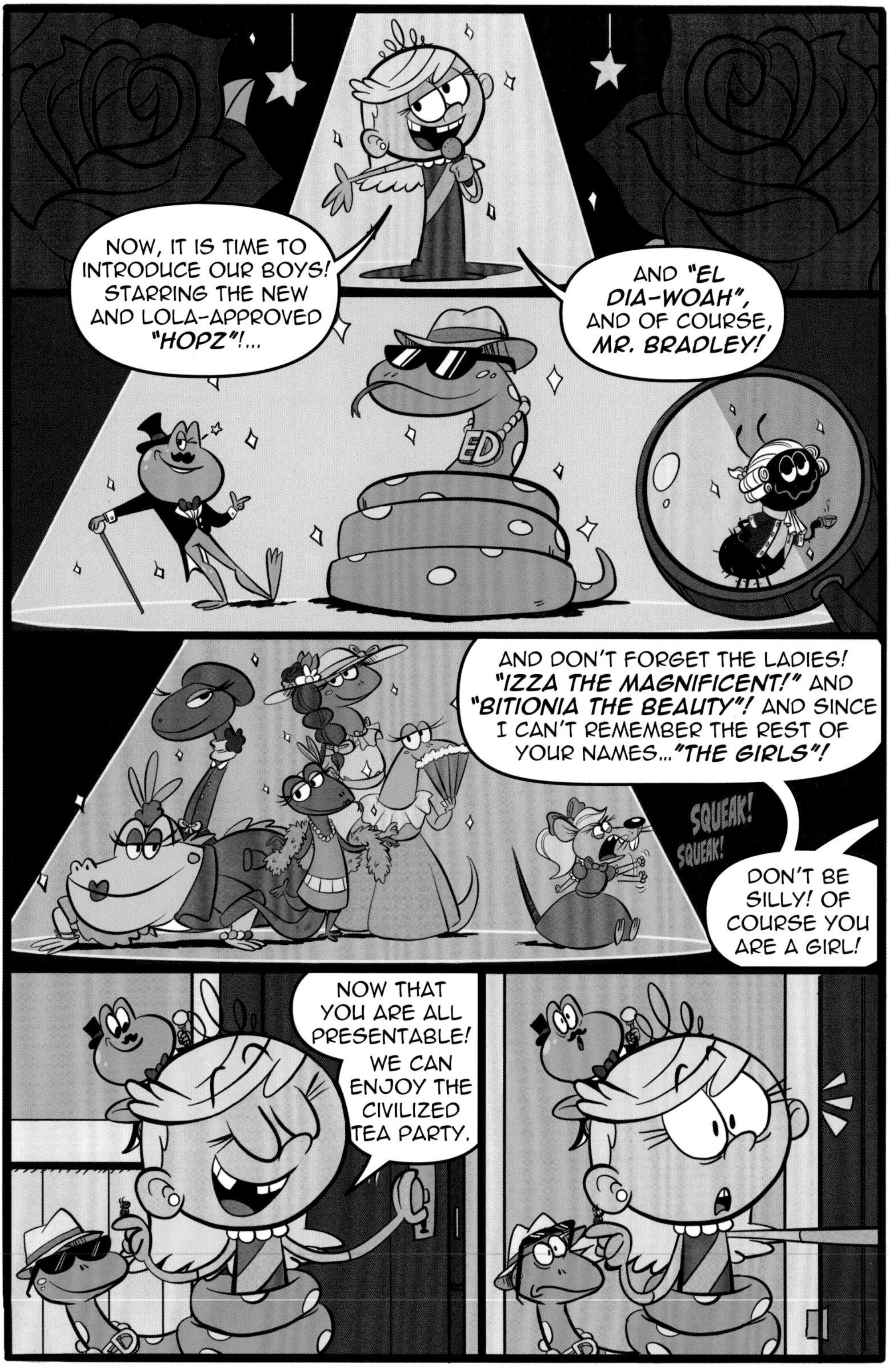
NOW, IT IS TIME TO INTRODUCE OUR BOYS! STARRING THE NEW AND LOLA-APPROVED "HOPZ"!...
AND "EL DIA-WOAH", AND OF COURSE, MR. BRADLEY!
ED
AND DON'T FORGET THE LADIES! "IZZA THE MAGNIFICENT!" AND "BITIONIA THE BEAUTY"! AND SINCE I CAN'T REMEMBER THE REST OF YOUR NAMES..."THE GIRLS"!
SQUEAK!
SQUEAK!
DON'T BE SILLY! OF COURSE YOU ARE A GIRL!
NOW THAT YOU ARE ALL PRESENTABLE! WE CAN ENJOY THE CIVILIZED TEA PARTY.

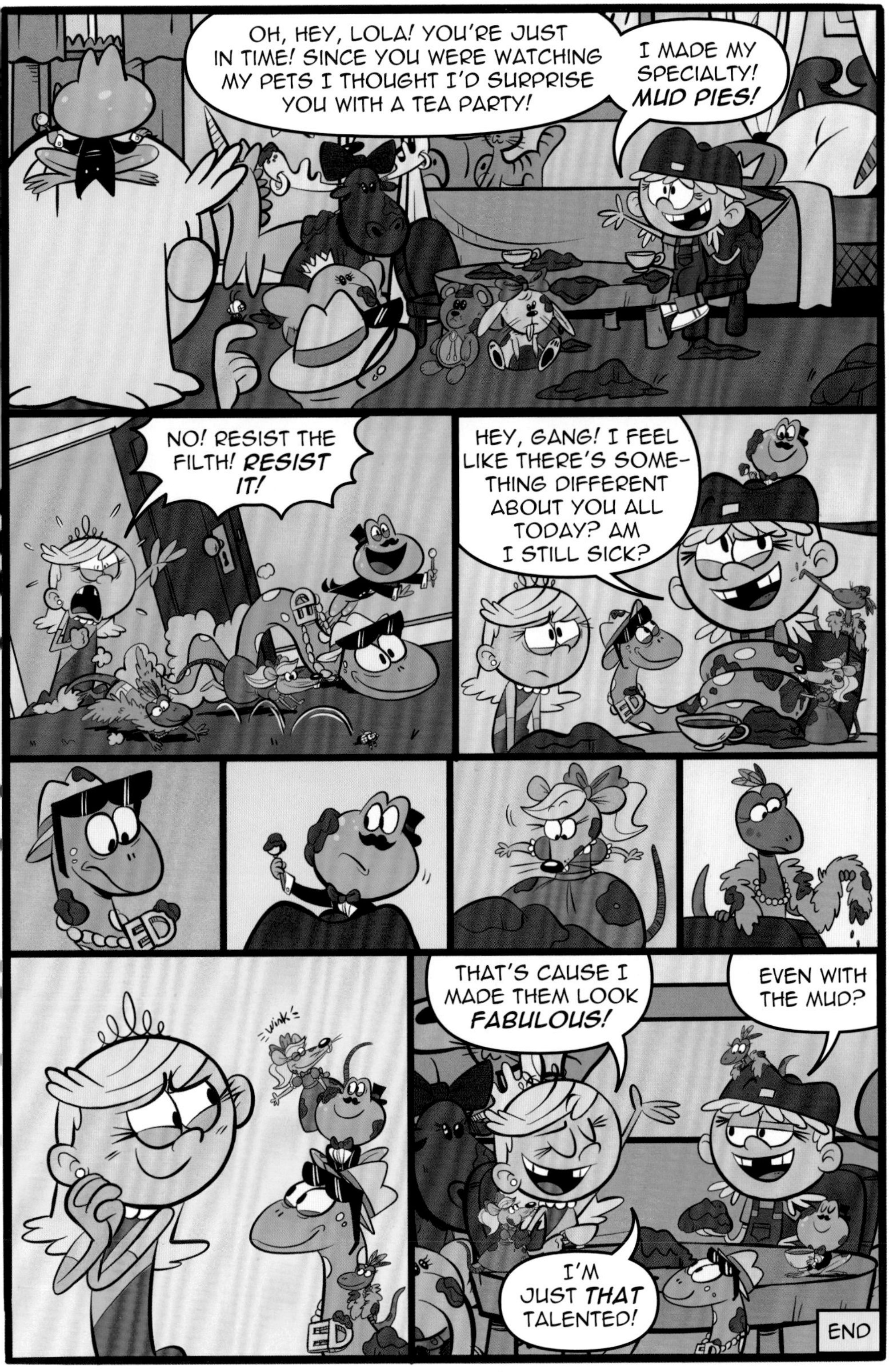
OH, HEY, LOLA! YOU'RE JUST IN TIME! SINCE YOU WERE WATCHING MY PETS I THOUGHT I'D SURPRISE YOU WITH A TEA PARTY!
I MADE MY SPECIALTY! MUD PIES!
NO! RESIST THE FILTH! RESIST IT!
HEY, GANG! I FEEL LIKE THERE'S SOME-THING DIFFERENT ABOUT YOU ALL TODAY? AM I STILL SICK?
wink
THAT'S CAUSE I MADE THEM LOOK FABULOUS!
EVEN WITH THE MUD?
I'M JUST THAT TALENTED!
END

"DIAGNOSIS: LOUD"

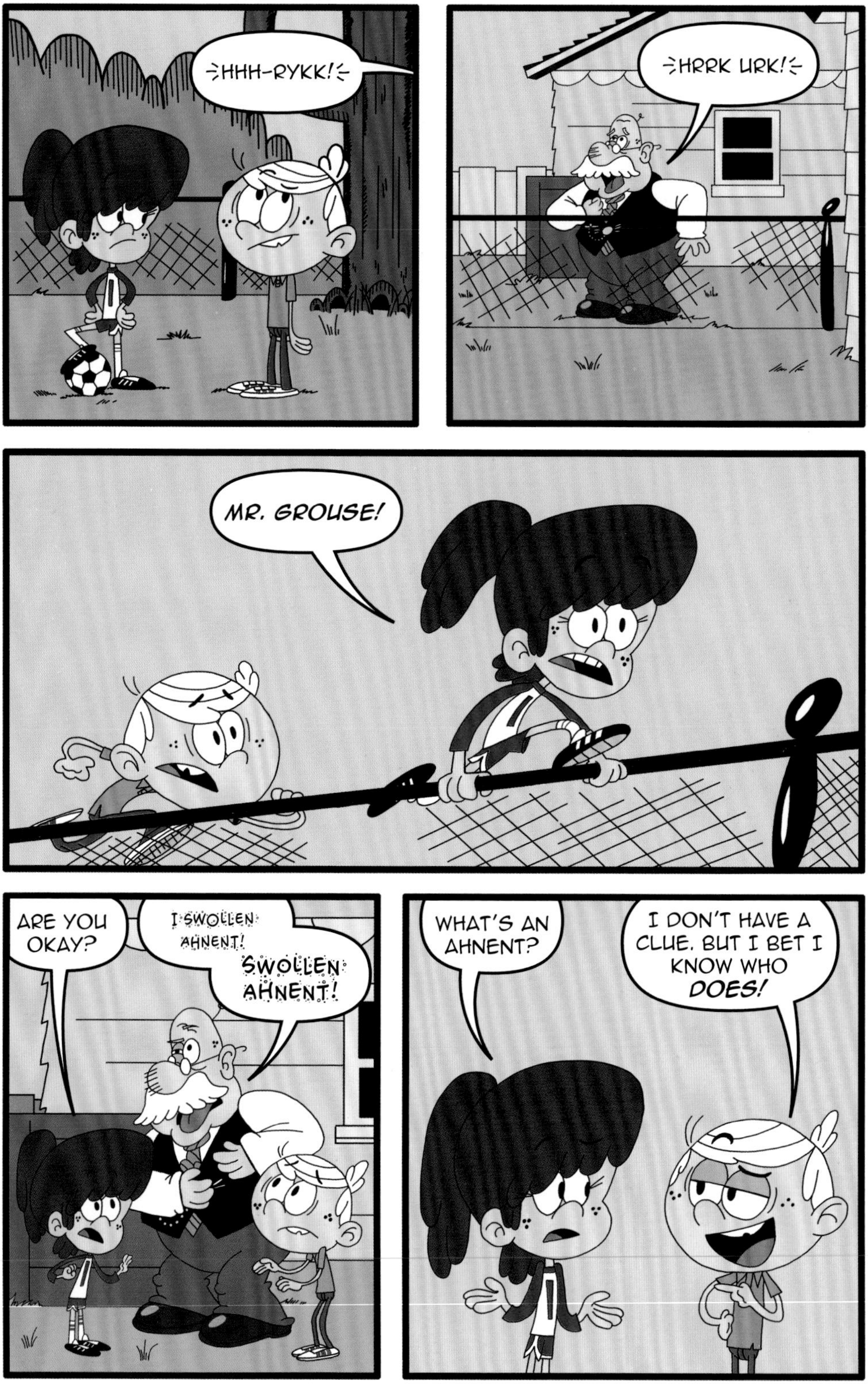

HHH-RYKK!
HRRK URK!
MR. GROUSE!
ARE YOU OKAY?
I SWOLLEN AHNENT!
SWOLLEN AHNENT!
WHAT'S AN AHNENT?
I DON'T HAVE A CLUE. BUT I BET I KNOW WHO DOES!

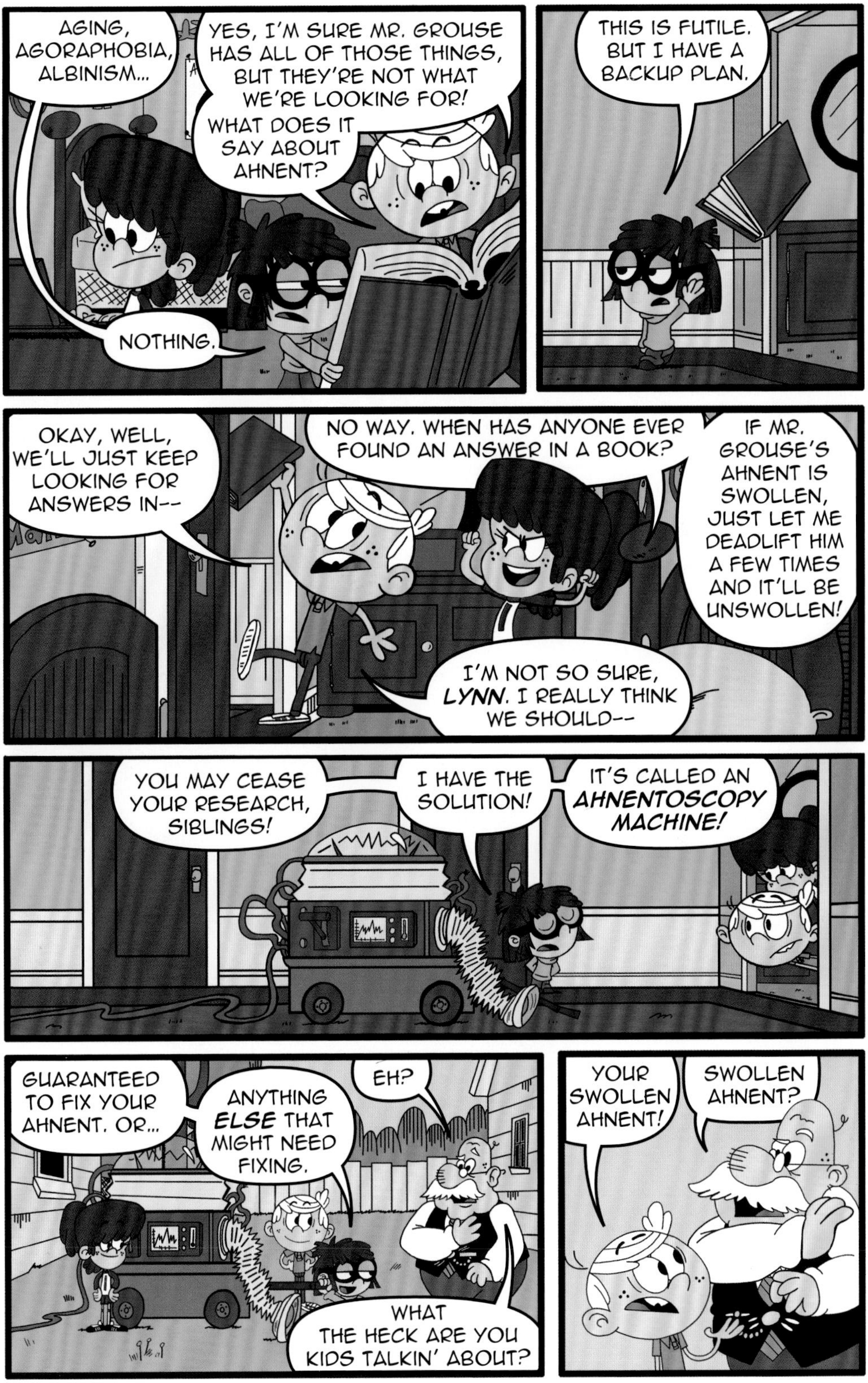
AGING, AGORAPHOBIA, ALBINISM...
YES, I'M SURE MR. GROUSE HAS ALL OF THOSE THINGS, BUT THEY'RE NOT WHAT WE'RE LOOKING FOR!
WHAT DOES IT SAY ABOUT AHNENT?
NOTHING.
THIS IS FUTILE. BUT I HAVE A BACKUP PLAN.
OKAY, WELL, WE'LL JUST KEEP LOOKING FOR ANSWERS IN--
NO WAY. WHEN HAS ANYONE EVER FOUND AN ANSWER IN A BOOK?
IF MR. GROUSE'S AHNENT IS SWOLLEN, JUST LET ME DEADLIFT HIM A FEW TIMES AND IT'LL BE UNSWOLLEN!
I'M NOT SO SURE, *LYNN*. I REALLY THINK WE SHOULD--
YOU MAY CEASE YOUR RESEARCH, SIBLINGS!
I HAVE THE SOLUTION!
IT'S CALLED AN ***AHNENTOSCOPY MACHINE!***
GUARANTEED TO FIX YOUR AHNENT. OR...
ANYTHING ***ELSE*** THAT MIGHT NEED FIXING.
EH?
WHAT THE HECK ARE YOU KIDS TALKIN' ABOUT?
YOUR SWOLLEN AHNENT!
SWOLLEN AHNENT?

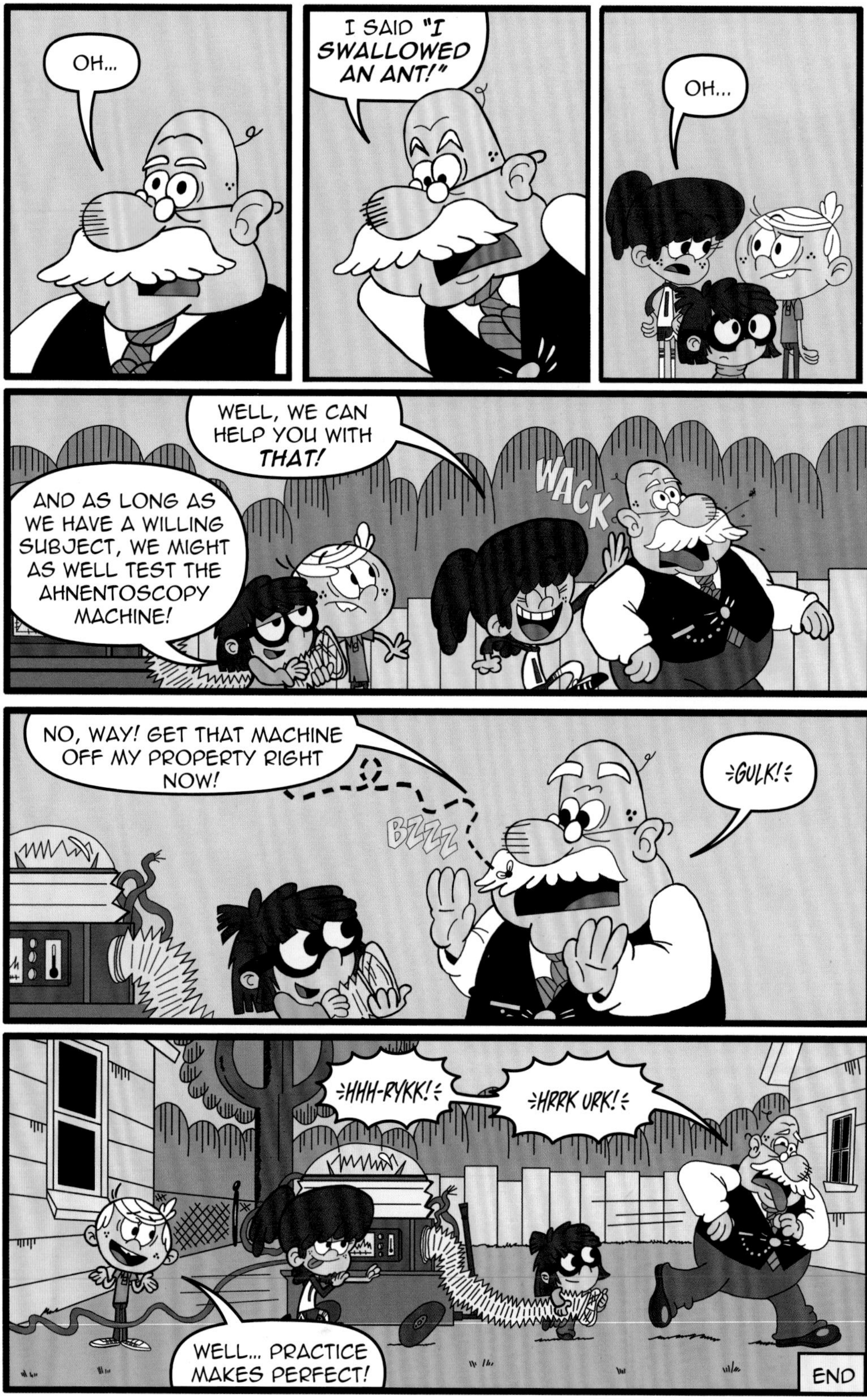
OH...
I SAID "I SWALLOWED AN ANT!"
OH...
WELL, WE CAN HELP YOU WITH THAT!
WACK
AND AS LONG AS WE HAVE A WILLING SUBJECT, WE MIGHT AS WELL TEST THE AHNENTOSCOPY MACHINE!
NO, WAY! GET THAT MACHINE OFF MY PROPERTY RIGHT NOW!
BZZZ
GULK!
HHH-RYKK!
HRRK URK!
WELL... PRACTICE MAKES PERFECT!
END

"CAKE-ENSTEIN'S MONSTER"

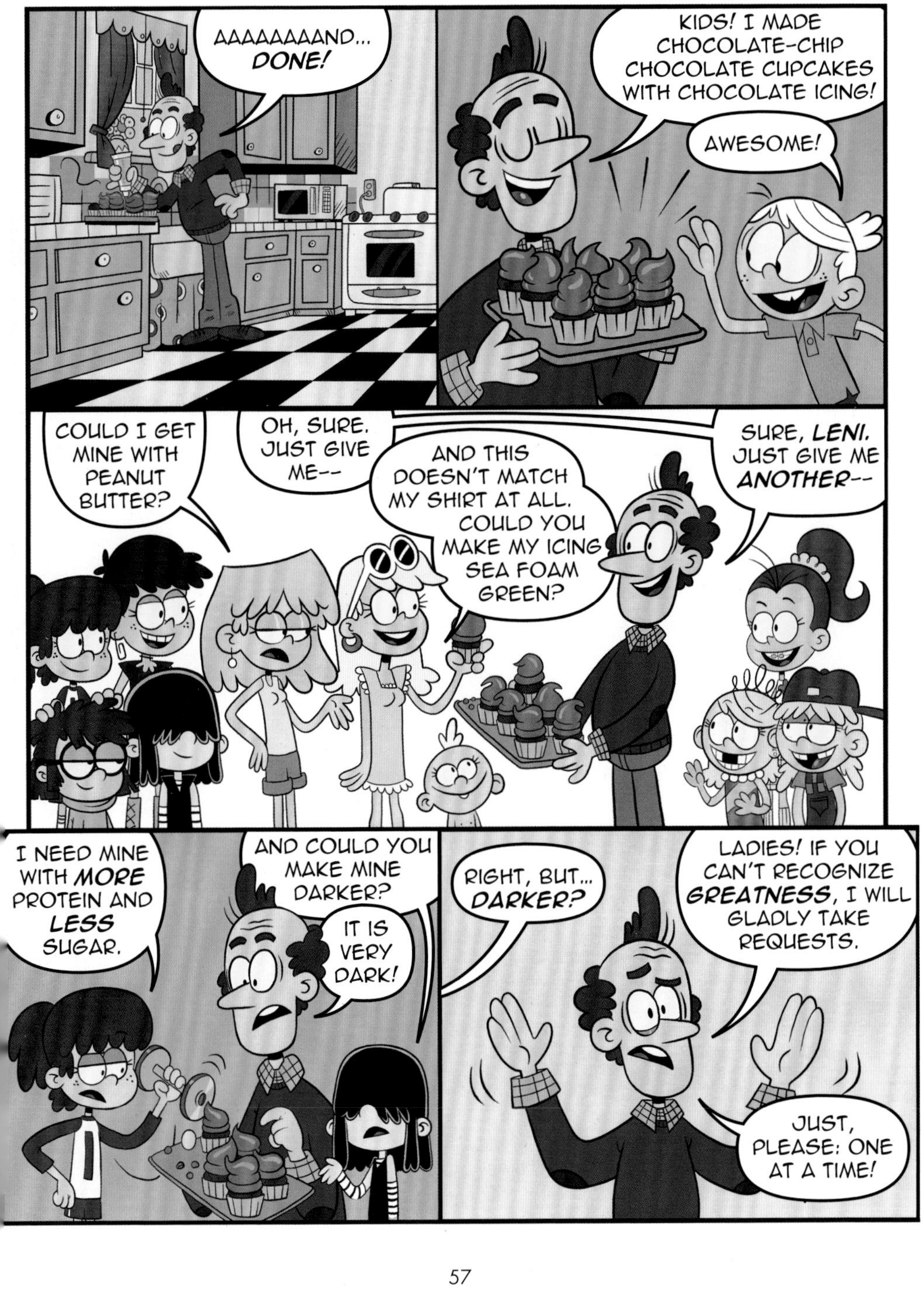
AAAAAAAAND...
DONE!
KIDS! I MADE CHOCOLATE-CHIP CHOCOLATE CUPCAKES WITH CHOCOLATE ICING!
AWESOME!
COULD I GET MINE WITH PEANUT BUTTER?
OH, SURE. JUST GIVE ME--
AND THIS DOESN'T MATCH MY SHIRT AT ALL. COULD YOU MAKE MY ICING SEA FOAM GREEN?
SURE, LENI. JUST GIVE ME ANOTHER--
I NEED MINE WITH MORE PROTEIN AND LESS SUGAR.
AND COULD YOU MAKE MINE DARKER?
IT IS VERY DARK!
RIGHT, BUT... DARKER?
LADIES! IF YOU CAN'T RECOGNIZE GREATNESS, I WILL GLADLY TAKE REQUESTS.
JUST, PLEASE: ONE AT A TIME!

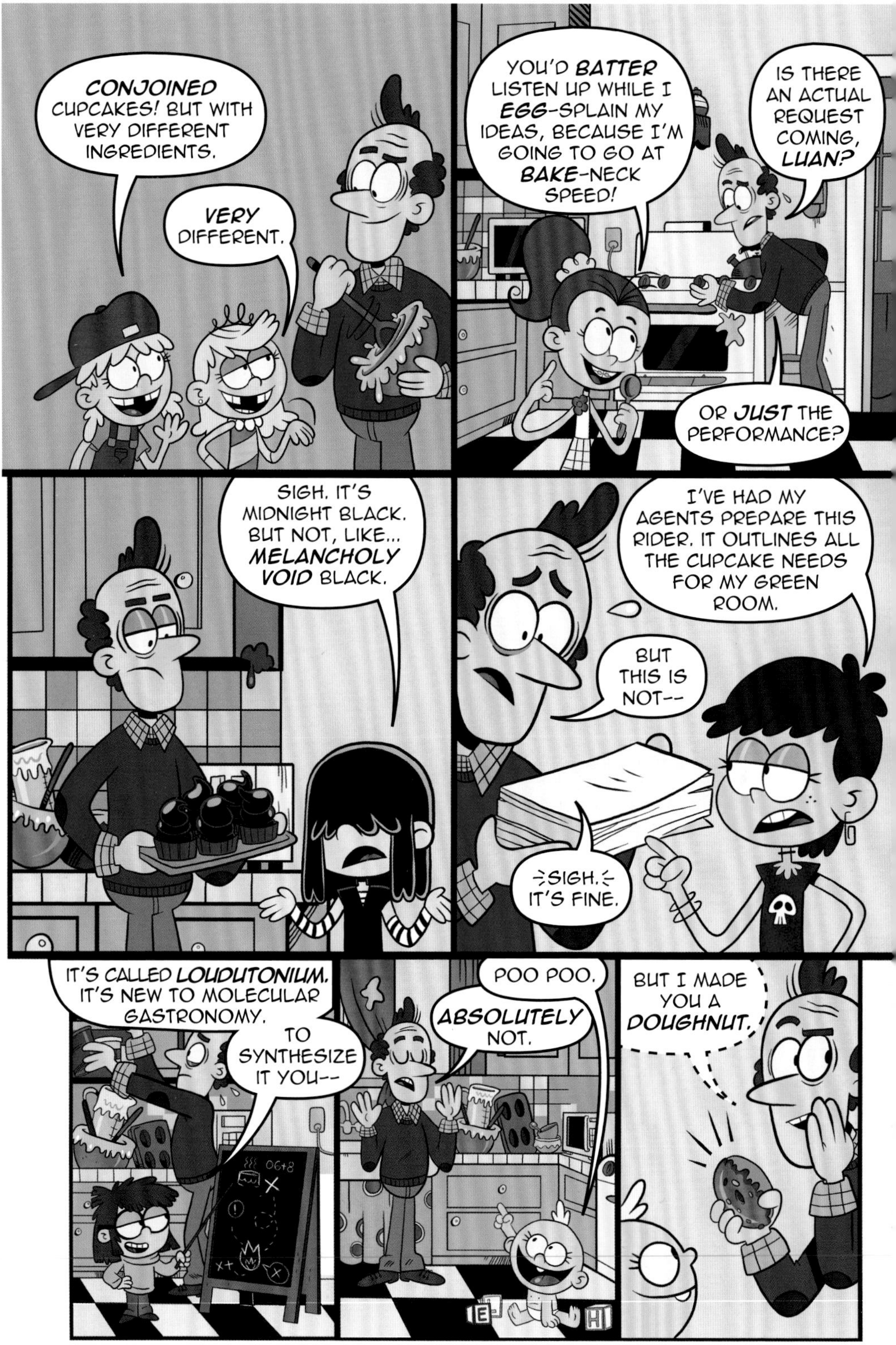
CONJOINED CUPCAKES! BUT WITH VERY DIFFERENT INGREDIENTS.
VERY DIFFERENT.
YOU'D BATTER LISTEN UP WHILE I EGG-SPLAIN MY IDEAS, BECAUSE I'M GOING TO GO AT BAKE-NECK SPEED!
IS THERE AN ACTUAL REQUEST COMING, LUAN?
OR JUST THE PERFORMANCE?
SIGH. IT'S MIDNIGHT BLACK. BUT NOT, LIKE... MELANCHOLY VOID BLACK.
I'VE HAD MY AGENTS PREPARE THIS RIDER. IT OUTLINES ALL THE CUPCAKE NEEDS FOR MY GREEN ROOM.
BUT THIS IS NOT--
SIGH. IT'S FINE.
IT'S CALLED LOUDUTONIUM. IT'S NEW TO MOLECULAR GASTRONOMY.
TO SYNTHESIZE IT YOU--
POO POO.
ABSOLUTELY NOT.
BUT I MADE YOU A DOUGHNUT.

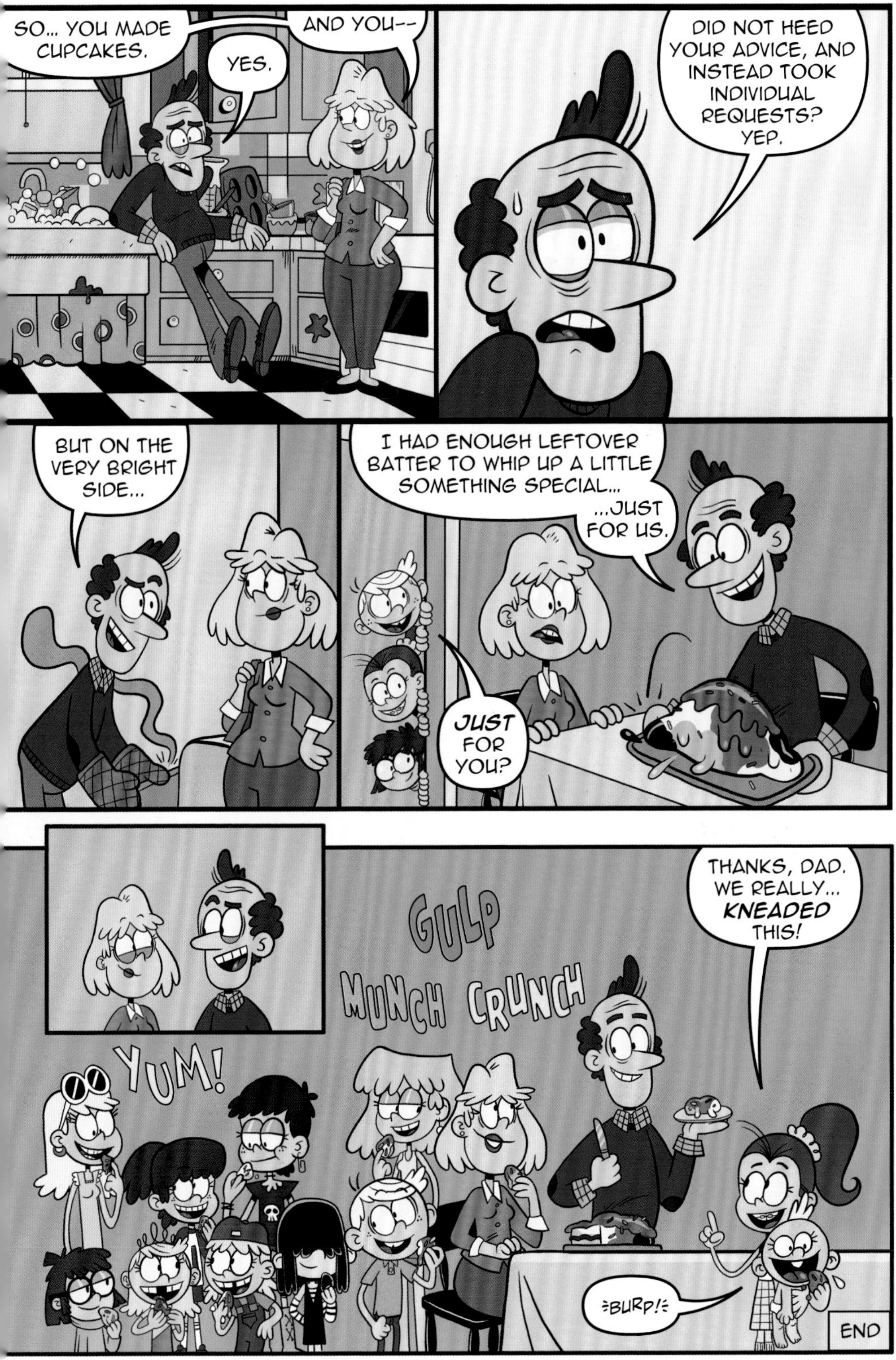

SO... YOU MADE CUPCAKES.
YES.
AND YOU--
DID NOT HEED YOUR ADVICE, AND INSTEAD TOOK INDIVIDUAL REQUESTS? YEP.
BUT ON THE VERY BRIGHT SIDE...
I HAD ENOUGH LEFTOVER BATTER TO WHIP UP A LITTLE SOMETHING SPECIAL...
...JUST FOR US.
JUST FOR YOU?
GULP
MUNCH CRUNCH
THANKS, DAD. WE REALLY... KNEADED THIS!
YUM!
BURP!
END

Warm up with an exclusive preview of THE LOUD HOUSE SUMMER SPECIAL!

"LUCY'S SUMMER FASHION TIPS"

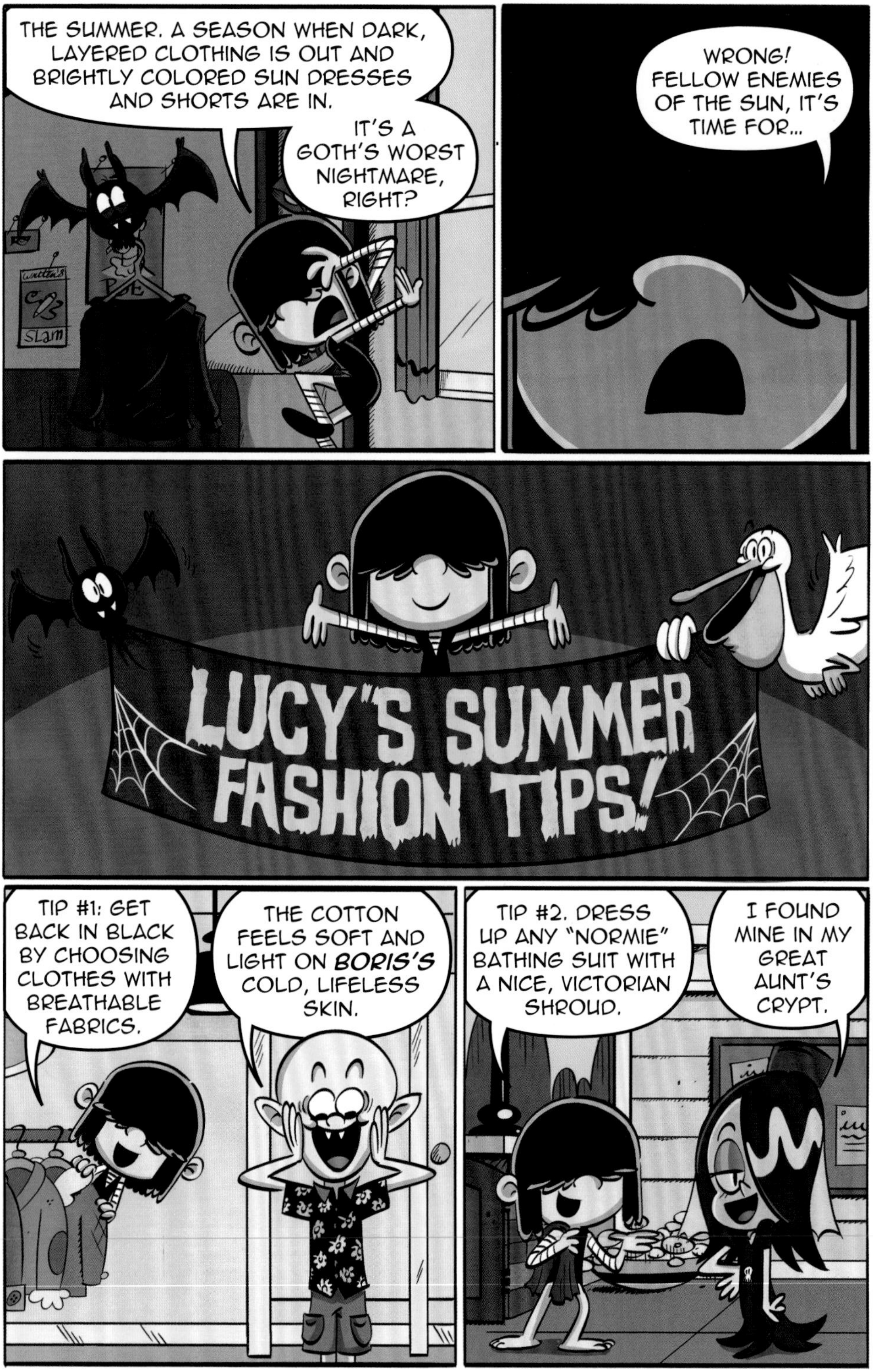
THE SUMMER. A SEASON WHEN DARK, LAYERED CLOTHING IS OUT AND BRIGHTLY COLORED SUN DRESSES AND SHORTS ARE IN.
IT'S A GOTH'S WORST NIGHTMARE, RIGHT?
WRONG! FELLOW ENEMIES OF THE SUN, IT'S TIME FOR...
LUCY'S SUMMER FASHION TIPS!
TIP #1: GET BACK IN BLACK BY CHOOSING CLOTHES WITH BREATHABLE FABRICS.
THE COTTON FEELS SOFT AND LIGHT ON *BORIS'S* COLD, LIFELESS SKIN.
TIP #2. DRESS UP ANY "NORMIE" BATHING SUIT WITH A NICE, VICTORIAN SHROUD.
I FOUND MINE IN MY GREAT AUNT'S CRYPT.

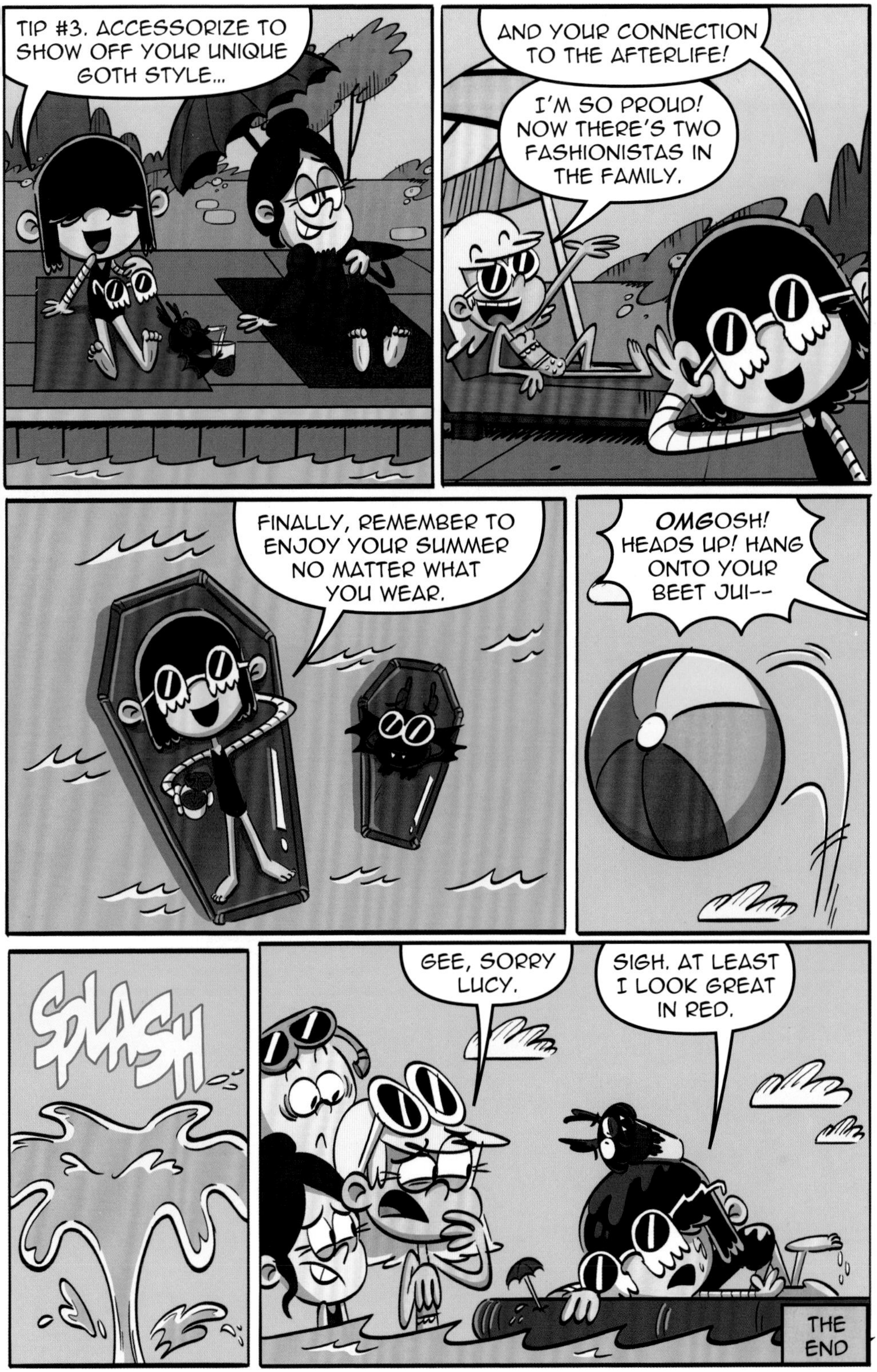
TIP #3. ACCESSORIZE TO SHOW OFF YOUR UNIQUE GOTH STYLE...
AND YOUR CONNECTION TO THE AFTERLIFE!
I'M SO PROUD! NOW THERE'S TWO FASHIONISTAS IN THE FAMILY.
FINALLY, REMEMBER TO ENJOY YOUR SUMMER NO MATTER WHAT YOU WEAR.
OMGOSH! HEADS UP! HANG ONTO YOUR BEET JUI--
SPLASH
GEE, SORRY LUCY.
SIGH. AT LEAST I LOOK GREAT IN RED.
THE END

Be sure to pick up THE LOUD HOUSE SUMMER SPECIAL available wherever books are sold, coming this summer!

Check in with THE CASAGRANDES in THE CASAGRANDES SPECIAL "We're All Familia"!

"THE GREAT ESCAPE"

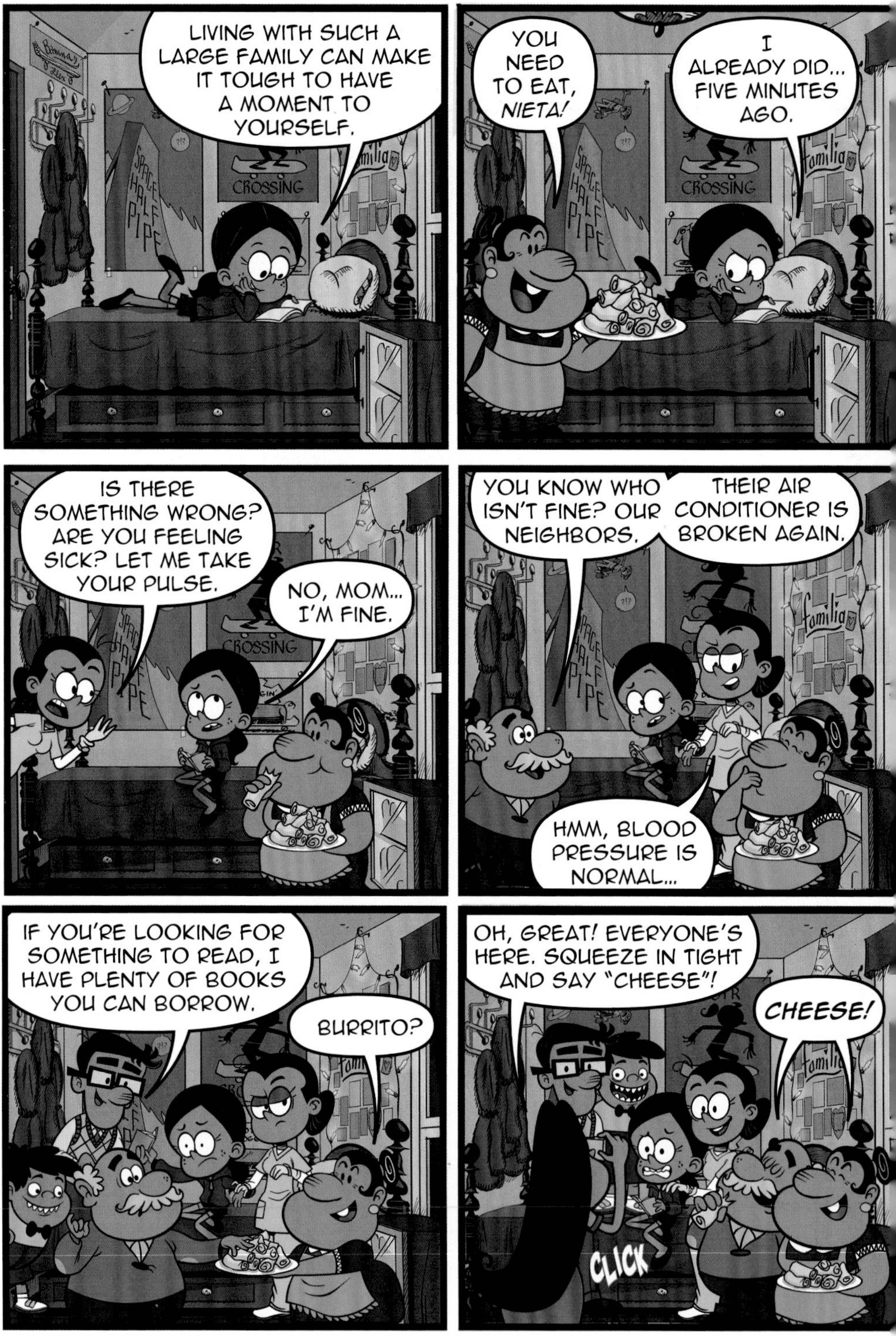
LIVING WITH SUCH A LARGE FAMILY CAN MAKE IT TOUGH TO HAVE A MOMENT TO YOURSELF.
YOU NEED TO EAT, NIETA!
I ALREADY DID... FIVE MINUTES AGO.
IS THERE SOMETHING WRONG? ARE YOU FEELING SICK? LET ME TAKE YOUR PULSE.
NO, MOM... I'M FINE.
YOU KNOW WHO ISN'T FINE? OUR NEIGHBORS.
THEIR AIR CONDITIONER IS BROKEN AGAIN.
HMM, BLOOD PRESSURE IS NORMAL...
IF YOU'RE LOOKING FOR SOMETHING TO READ, I HAVE PLENTY OF BOOKS YOU CAN BORROW.
BURRITO?
OH, GREAT! EVERYONE'S HERE. SQUEEZE IN TIGHT AND SAY "CHEESE"!
CHEESE!
CLICK

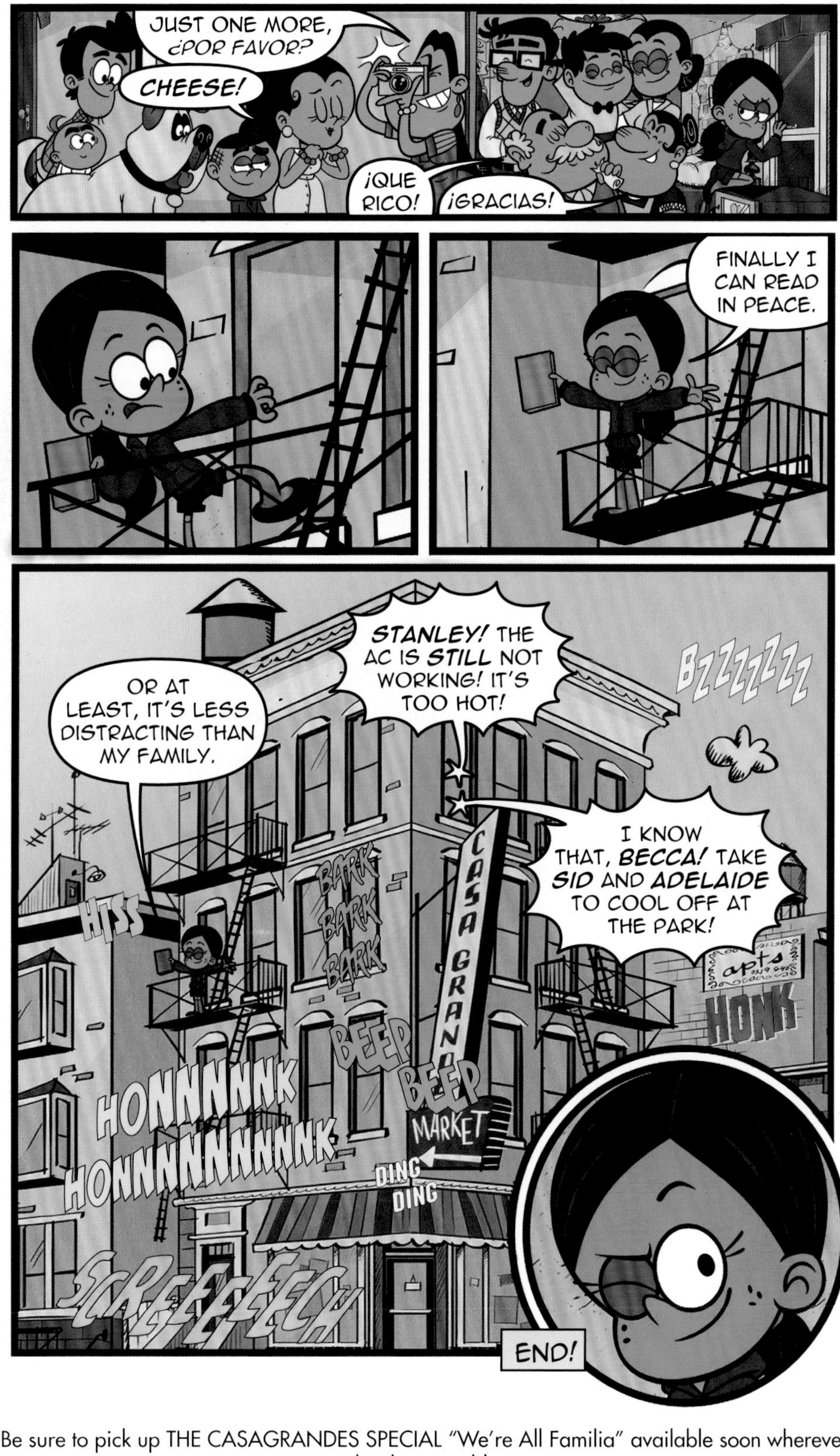
JUST ONE MORE, ¿POR FAVOR?
CHEESE!
¡QUE RICO!
¡GRACIAS!
FINALLY I CAN READ IN PEACE.
OR AT LEAST, IT'S LESS DISTRACTING THAN MY FAMILY.
STANLEY! THE AC IS STILL NOT WORKING! IT'S TOO HOT!
BZZZZZZZ
I KNOW THAT, BECCA! TAKE SID AND ADELAIDE TO COOL OFF AT THE PARK!
HISS
BARK
BARK
BARK
HONK
BEEP
BEEP
HONNNNNK
HONNNNNNNNNK
MARKET
DING
DING
SCREEEEECH
END!

Be sure to pick up THE CASAGRANDES SPECIAL "We're All Familia" available soon wherever books are sold!

WATCH OUT FOR PAPERCUTZ™

Welcome to the tantalizing twelfth THE LOUD HOUSE graphic novel "The Case of the Stolen Drawers," from Papercutz, those well-attired types dedicated to publishing great graphic novels for all ages. I'm Jim Salicrup, Editor-in-Chief and part-time gag writer for Luan Loud. One of the best "problems" any publisher can have is people complaining that you don't come out with enough books featuring their favorite characters. At Papercutz, we're bombarded by requests for more of THE LOUD HOUSE graphic novels. So, we heard you, and we listened, and we're happy to announce the following special Papercutz graphic novels.

First off, there's THE LOUD HOUSE SUMMER SPECIAL. Summer truly is special. School's out and there's plenty of time for fun. Not that that Loud family don't have fun all year 'round, but if you live somewhere where it snows in the winter, those hot summer beach days are precious. So, Lincoln and his sisters Lori, Leni, Luna, Lynn, Luan, Lucy (yes, even Lucy!), Lola, Lana, and Lily can't wait to hit the beach or chill out by the pool, or just look for a delicious icy treat to beat the heat. The Casagrandes are included in the fun as well. Ronnie Anne, Bobby, and the rest of their extended family are searching for foolproof ways of handling the scorching summer in the big city. This extra-special graphic novel features a mix of new stories and past favorites from THE LOUD HOUSE graphic novel series.

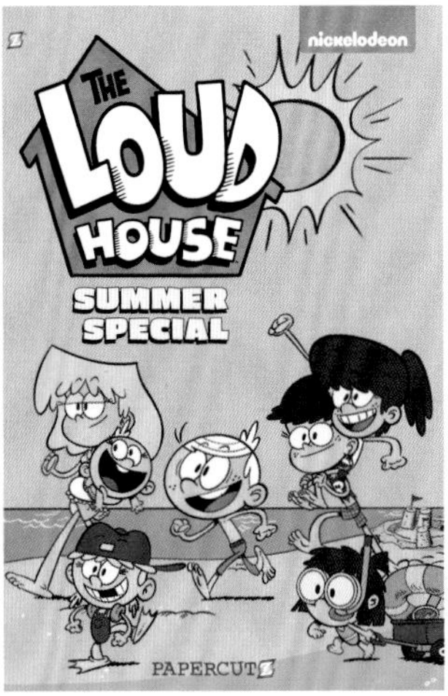
nickelodeon
THE LOUD HOUSE
SUMMER SPECIAL
PAPERCUTZ

And speaking of THE CASAGRANDES, guess who are starring in a special graphic novel all of their own? That's right! Papercutz presents the very first THE CASAGRANDES graphic novel. When Lincoln Loud's good friend Ronnie Anne, and Lori's boyfriend (Ronnie Anne's brother) Bobby, and their mother, Maria, moved away from Royal Oaks to an apartment in the Big City, above their abuelo's (grandpaprents) mercado, it was a big change. Now they're with the kid's abuelos, Hector and Rosa, as well as Rosa's brother, Carlos, his wife, Frida, and their four kids, Carlota, CJ (Carlos Jr.), Carl, and Carlitos, not to mention their pets, Lalo (the dog) and Sergio (the bird). Likewise, this graphic novel features new stories and past favorites which appeared in THE LOUD HOUSE graphic novels.

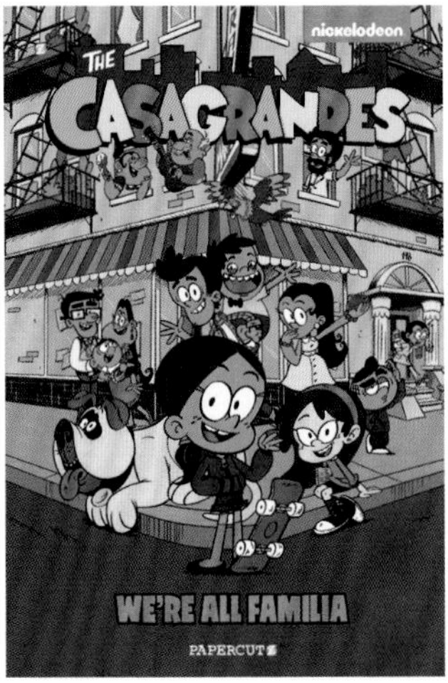
nickelodeon
THE CASAGRANDES
WE'RE ALL FAMILIA
PAPERCUTZ

We've even included a preview story from each SPECIAL in this very graphic novel — so check it out! And if those two graphic novels, plus the shows themselves on Nickelodeon, can't satisfy your cravings for more of THE LOUD HOUSE, don't worry. Coming soon is the all-new THE LOUD HOUSE #13 "Lucy Rolls the Dice"! Find out what happens when a storm knocks out the electricity at the Loud house and the kids have to find new ways to entertain themselves. With these eleven kids, we're sure they'll come up with a few surprises.

Thanks, JIM

STAY IN TOUCH!

EMAIL:	salicrup@papercutz.com
WEB:	papercutz.com
TWITTER:	@papercutzgn
INSTAGRAM:	@papercutzgn
FACEBOOK:	PAPERCUTZGRAPHICNOVELS
FANMAIL:	Papercutz, 160 Broadway, Suite 700, East Wing, New York, NY 10038

Go to papercutz.com and sign up for the free Papercutz e-newsletter!

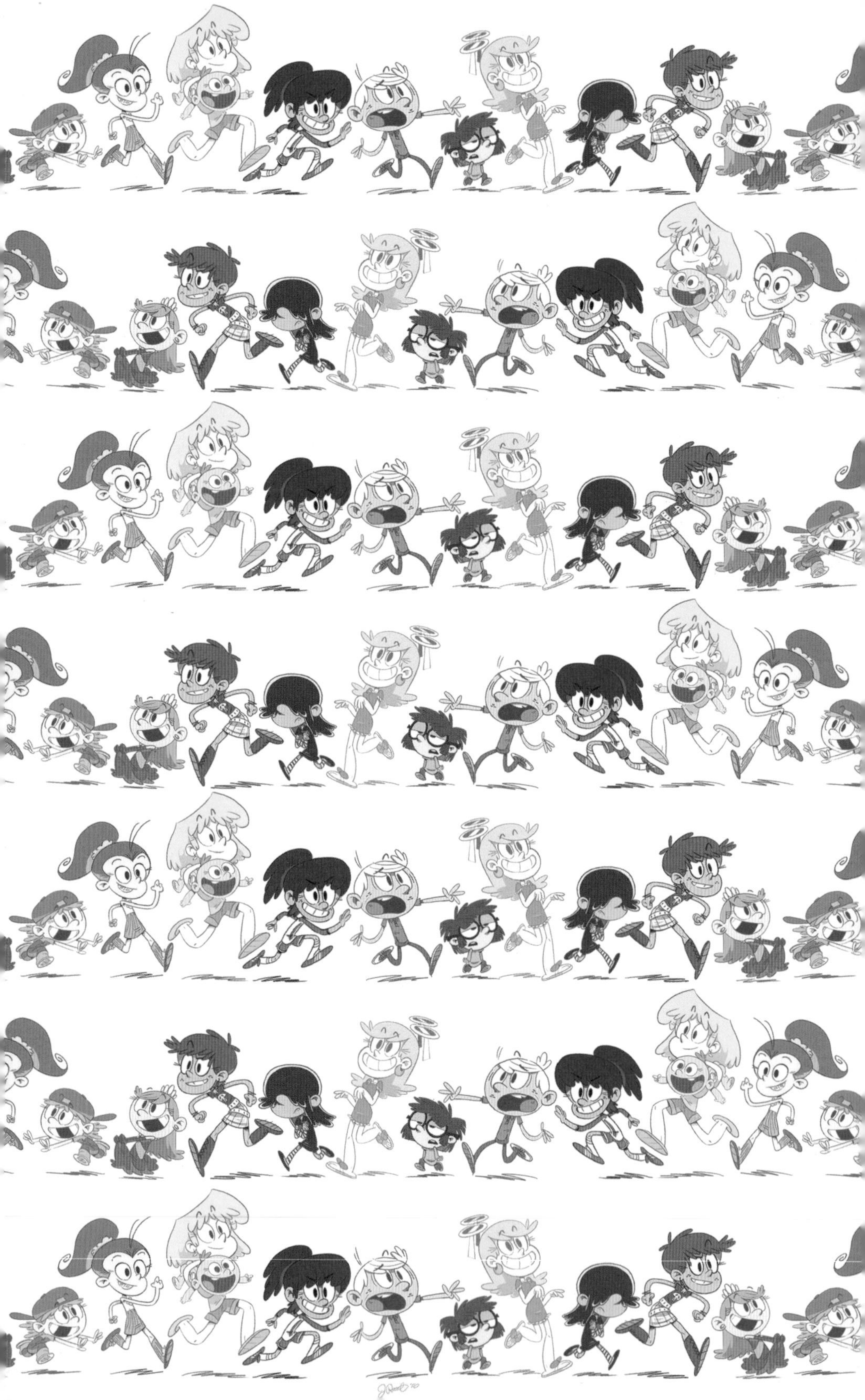